FAMILY CIRCLE

CLAIRE ST. JOHN

AMANDA UMFRESS

TOUCHPOINT FAITH **f**

Inspirational. Positive. Encouraging.

Megan,

U hope you enjoy the book.
Best Wishes,
amanda Umfress

FAMILY CIRCLE: CLAIRE ST. JOHN
By Amanda Umfress
Published by TouchPoint Faith
An imprint of TouchPoint Press
Brookland, AR 72417
www.touchpointpress.com

ISBN-13: 978-1-952816-93-2

Editor: Kimberly Coghlan
Cover Design: David Ter-Avanesyan, Ter33Design

Visit the author's website at amandaumfress.com

First Edition

Printed in the United States of America.

To my husband and children—Jeff, Logan, Allie, and Harper. Thank you for always believing in me.

To my dear friends: Debbie Moore for being the first reader and Amanda Austin for answering those numerous text messages to lend me her medical expertise. Thank you!

And to Pawpaw Gene, Meme, Nana, Paw, and Mawmaw Kay. Thank you for making sure that faith was always and continues to be an important part of my life.

CHAPTER ONE

IN THE CHAPEL, CLAIRE ST. JOHN held a raveling hymnbook in one hand while the other hand rested on her stomach. Bridging old and new, the fresh sun beamed through the stained-glass windows, generating a kaleidoscope on the aged, mahogany pulpit. Vibrant flowers throughout the chapel fostered spring. Claire closed her eyes and inhaled deeply, taking in the flowers' aroma. She listened to the organ's melodies, and the congregation's voices hummed below the joyful music of praise.

Though she tried to focus on the moment, her thoughts drifted toward the strange twinges in her lower abdomen. Today marked Claire's twelfth week of pregnancy with her first child. As the music ended, she placed her hymnbook into the holder and lowered herself down onto the pew beside her husband Jack. She watched as the pastor took his place behind the wooden pulpit.

Claire studied Pastor David Mize. A tall man in his early thirties with sandy blonde hair that tipped his white shirt collar, he was originally from Kentucky and had joined Victory Baptist Church in Nashville ten years ago, long before she and Jack became members. Since joining the church five years ago, Jack and Claire's friendship had blossomed with David, his wife Macy, and their three young daughters. In fact, Macy had become her best friend.

Claire's gaze shifted toward Macy, who sat on the first pew with her Bible on her lap. Dressed in a red striped dress with a white shawl to protect her from the spring chill, her sandy blonde curls soaked up the colors of the chapel like sponges, and the light illuminated her freckles, which danced along the bridge of her nose. At thirty-two, Macy was beautiful, and she, David, and their children portrayed the perfect Christian family. Claire felt her cheeks redden as a familiar pang of envy rushed through her body. She shook her head as if to wash it away, and she rubbed her belly again and smiled at Jack. Pastor David's voice broke through Claire's thoughts, and he spoke clearly as he addressed the congregation.

"Good morning everyone! What a glorious day it is to be here together. The music this morning was a blessing, and I know I won't be able to compete with such wonderfulness but bear with me."

A soft chuckle echoed through the congregation, and Claire forced herself to smile and focus on the preacher's words.

David smiled pleasantly and continued. "Please turn your bibles to Revelations 21:4 for our scripture reading today. 'And God shall wipe away all tears from their eyes and there shall be no more death, neither sorrow, nor crying, neither shall there be any more pain: for the former things are passed away.'"

The verse forced Claire to swallow loudly, and Jack

cast a worried glance toward her. She smiled at Jack and focused once again on David as he lowered his bible and turned his attention to the congregation.

"We all face a time in our lives that leaves us wondering why sorrow and pain exist. Maybe you often think, 'Why me?' Or maybe you think, 'This isn't fair. I am a Christian; bad things are not supposed to happen to me.'"

A few "Amens" rang out through the congregation.

David held up his hand and looked onto his congregation. "Even when we are facing the toughest challenges, know that God will be by your side. He is your rock, and you need to remember to lean upon him. Give all your worries, sorrows, fears, and anger to him."

Some within the congregation spoke "Amen." Claire nodded silently.

David paused, allowing the congregation's voices to silence.

"Let's pray," David said. "Our Father which art in heaven, hallowed be Your name. Your kingdom come, Your will be done, on Earth as it is in heaven. Give us this day our daily bread, and forgive us our debts, as we also have forgiven our debtors. And lead us not into temptation but deliver us from evil."

An echo of "Amens" rang out from the congregation as Pastor David ended his prayer.

CHAPTER TWO

As CLAIRE TRIED TO FOCUS ON the pastor, a stabbing pain radiated throughout her abdomen. Even though this was her first pregnancy, she knew the pain was not normal. A flash of panic slowly crept up her spine, as a wave of nausea pooled in her stomach. *What's happening?* Claire silently thought. She swallowed as a fear gripped her heart. David continued to preach.

As the pain intensified, she shifted uncomfortably in her seat with an effort to ease the agony. The readjustment didn't work, and with a grimace, Claire looked over to her husband. Jack's face donned a peaceful expression that left his brown eyes shimmering and his chocolate, curly hair haphazardly bordering his brow. He appeared to be absorbed in the message, oblivious to her unease.

As the pains continued to circulate, Claire leaned over to Jack and whispered quietly, "Jack." He didn't immediately respond. She nudged him gently with her elbow, trying not to interrupt the Sunday morning service. "Jack, I need to go to the restroom."

He leaned his head gently toward her appearing to notice her uneasy expression. "You okay?" Jack whispered.

Claire tried to clear her panicked expression and half-heartily smiled for his sake. "Yes, I believe so. I'm going to go to the restroom."

She stood and turned sideways to slide to the end of the aging pew. As she did, her blue, satin skirt caught on the corner of the hymnal holder. She shifted slightly to free her skirt, only to create a stir of noise. Several nearby congregation members looked her way, and Claire smiled gently to the onlookers. Finally free, she walked down the aisle toward the double doors at the back of the room.

Why did we decide to sit on the third pew today? We should've just sat on the last row like last Sunday. Why did I have to suggest we move closer to the pulpit?

Claire knew the pain warranted a restroom visit, but a sliver of embarrassment fatigued her mind as she walked down the aisle. She grabbed the brass handles and pushed the mahogany doors. As the heavy doors opened, a slight breeze crossed her face. She glanced at the hallway from left to right. Since it was mid-service, the hallway was empty, and she was thankful for that, as she needed the solitude.

As Claire walked down the narrow hall toward the restroom, she heard children's laughter filling the hall from the nursery. She closed her eyes to take in the moment. *Lord, give me strength to understand what is happening. I pray it's nothing, Dear Lord. I pray you will take this fear away. Wrap your loving arms around me and my child.*

As she came to the bathroom door, she inhaled a long breath as another sharp pain riveted through her body. Claire pushed open the door, and a rush of warmth hit her face. She glanced around and noticed the small heater sitting in the corner. She selected the first stall, closed the brown door, latched the metal slide lock, and sat down.

Claire inhaled slowly as she looked down at her panties. Then she gasped aloud. "No, that's not possible."

Her heart sank at the site of blood on her panties. A war raged within her body as confusion, fear, and panic clouded her thoughts. *Breathe, Just Breathe.* Claire swallowed to control her panic.

She bowed her head and clasped her hands together. *Dear Lord, I'm scared and confused. Please help me understand what's happening. Please, please, protect my baby. I don't know your plan, but please Lord, let my baby be healthy.*

In the bathroom stall, Claire sank to the bathroom floor and cried. The tears flowed steadily as confusion engulfed her emotions.

Suddenly, she heard the door to the restroom open.

"Claire?" someone called out.

Though she wanted to respond, fear paralyzed Claire. A few moments later, Claire saw Macy's red pumps underneath the door, and with a struggle, she slowly rose to her feet as a gentle knock sounded.

"Claire, honey? Is everything alright?" Macy asked.

Claire's fingers shook as she reached the metal lock. She pushed back the tears as she unlocked the door and faced Macy. Claire could only imagine how she looked— puffy and swollen eyes, her face streaked with tears, and mascara running down her cheeks. She took the back of her palm and wiped her mouth while trying to sober her cries.

Macy froze. "Oh honey, please tell me what's wrong," Macy said gently.

"Macy, I think I might be losing my baby," Claire spoke raggedly through tears.

Macy gasped and cupped her hands over her mouth. Claire cried harder. Her sobs mixed with uneven, shallow breaths, and she felt a dizziness overcome her. Macy moved forward and put her arms around Claire, who immediately sank into her arms.

"Claire, honey. Everything's gonna be okay. I need you to calm down." Macy gently patted Claire's hair. "Why do you think you're having a miscarriage?"

Claire released herself from Macy's embrace and looked into her friend's eyes. She felt her mouth open, but the words struggled to form. "I . . . umm . . . there's blood and pain." She said between sobs. "What do I do? Macy, why is this happening? Why me? My baby, Macy. I can't lose this baby."

"Oh Claire, honey, take a deep breath, and let's not rush to assumptions." Macy's back straightened as an authoritative, protective emotion filled her. "First, we need to get Jack, and he can take you to the emergency room." Macy clucked her tongue against her cheek and nodded matter-of-factly as her perfectly groomed eyebrows burrowed deep. "Once they've looked you over, we'll know more." Macy nodded her head and stalled for a response.

Claire nodded her head.

"I'll find Jack. You stay here until I get him."

Again, Claire only nodded.

"David and I will follow y'all to the emergency room. Don't' worry, Claire. I have everything under control. I'll call Doctor Rogers and tell him you're headed there now," Macy gently said. "Oh, you're shivering. Come stand by the heater." Macy held her arm out to Claire, and together they slowly moved toward the heater. Each step intensified Claire's pain. "Okay. I'm going to find Jack. I'll be right back," she said.

When Macy opened the bathroom door, she saw Jack in the hallway.

"Macy. Have you seen Claire? When she didn't come back, I began to . . ." Jack froze. "What is it? What's wrong?"

Macy opened the bathroom door wider so Jack could see Claire.

Claire grabbed her abdomen to comfort her baby. She knew her husband's looks well enough to know that he was scared. His gentle face was set hard, and his green eyes were wide. His six-foot posture stiffened in a stance of protectiveness. "What's wrong, Claire?" he asked.

"It's the baby, Jack. Our baby," Claire finally said.

Jack, stunned, looked to Macy for clarification.

"Jack, we need to get her to the emergency room," Macy said.

He swallowed hard and nodded at Macy. "Claire, I've got you. It's going to be alright. I love you, honey," Jack said in a whisper.

Claire felt her feet come out from under her, and her head fell back against Jack's shoulder. His cologne filled her nostrils. She closed her eyes and inhaled gently to take the scent in deeper. As Jack carried her toward the church parking lot, she held on tightly, keeping her eyes closed.

"I got you Baybay. Don't worry," Jack whispered.

Claire heard Macy's red heels clicking against the pavement as she followed Claire and Jack to the car. Then, she heard the wooden doors to the Church open with a screech, and the breeze from the outside touched her cheeks. The Spring cold hit her face and made her inhale softly.

At the vehicle, Macy opened the passenger door, and Jack slid Claire into the car and buckled her seat belt. He shut the door.

Claire placed her hand on the window. Macy placed her hand on the opposite side. "It's all going to be okay, Claire. I love you," Macy mouthed.

"Macy, will you and David meet us there?" Jack asked.

"Of course. He should be about finished," Macy said. "I'll get Nana to take the kids with her, and we'll be on the way. I'm calling Dr. Rogers too," she said. Jack nodded, and Macy could see the fear on his face. "Jack, you need to show strength. Let the Lord handle the rest. Whatever is His will is, it will be done," Macy said.

Jack gave Macy a hug and rounded the front of the BMW to get into the driver's side. As he slid into the car, he put his hand on Claire's leg. "Claire, take a deep breath. Everything will be okay. I promise."

Jack started the engine and put the BMW into reverse. Macy backed away as Jack backed out of the parking spot.

CHAPTER THREE

HIS CELL PHONE RANG AS JACK SPED down the interstate toward Nashville Grace Hospital. He looked over at Claire as if waiting for instructions. "Honey, it's your mom. Should I take it, or do you want me to call her back?"

"Go ahead; take it," she said in a whisper.

Jack put his headphones in his ears. "Hello."

"Jack, how's my baby girl? Good Lord, have Mercy, I bout' had a heart attack when Macy called me. How is my grandshug?" Beth said in one breath.

Jack heard his father-in-law's deep throaty voice in the background. "Beth, give the boy a chance to answer. Take a breath for goodness sake."

"Mica, just hush and let me talk," Beth said in an aggravated tone. "Jack are ya there, honey?

"Yes, Beth I'm here," Jack replied.

"Jack, Oh Jack! My sweet Claire?"

Jack navigated the road as he listened to Beth.

"Jack, Oh my goodness. How is Claire?" Beth asked.

"Good Lord, Beth. You have asked that boy fifteen questions and haven't given him a chance to answer. Hand me the phone," Claire's dad interrupted from the background.

Jack heard the shifting of the phone. "Jack, son. Beth is just a basket case right now. I'm sorry."

"It's understandable, Mica. We're all worried."

"Son, tell me what Claire's symptoms are," Mica said using his physician, authoritative voice.

"She began having some pains in Church. She went to the restroom and found blood in her panties."

"No other symptoms?" Mica asked.

Jack looked over to Claire. "Honey, your dad is asking if you have any other symptoms?"

"No. Just pain and blood. That's all," she responded numbly.

"That's . . ." Jack began to say as Mica interrupted him.

"I heard her. Jack asked her if the blood was dark or bright red."

"Sir?" Jack asked, confused.

"Son, just ask her please," Mica said with authority.

"Claire, sweetheart. Your dad wants to know what color the blood was," Jack said reluctantly. He bit his bottom lip as a wave of nausea passed over him.

Claire slowly looked over at her husband. *Bless him, she thought.* Jack had one of the weakest stomachs. He was a brilliant man, and when he was younger, he had thoughts of going to medical school. But he couldn't handle the sight of blood. They both knew when this child came, Claire would have to be the parent to deal with any blood-related boo-boos. Claire breathed deeply as the thought made her remember where they were heading.

"Jack, again, what color is the blood?" Mica asked impatiently.

"Claire, the blood color?" Jack asked, his eyes not leaving the road.

"It was dark. Kinda maroonish, I suppose," she said.

"I heard her answer," Mica spoke before Jack could respond. Jack sighed.

"Dark is better than bright red, but she shouldn't be having pain. Jack, she may be having a miscarriage. Or it's possible that she has just overworked and stressed her body. Either way, you're doing the best thing by taking her to the emergency room."

Jack heard Beth crying in the background. "Mica, a miscarriage? She huffed through tears. The phone shifted hands again. "Both of you just hush all that talk now. I'm sure it's not that. My grandshug is going to be just fine. You wait and see," Beth said to reassure him.

"I hope you're right. We're just holding on to faith for a positive outcome," Jack said.

"Oh Jack, my heart's just aching for my baby girl," she said with a heavy sigh. "Macy called us a while ago, so we're already headed to the hospital, but you know Mica drives slower than Christmas."

"How far have y'all gotten?" Jack asked her.

"The last sign I saw said we were about fifty miles out from Nashville," she said with her southern drawl. "Don't even ask me why we took the slowest route." Beth snarled at her husband. "Well, you know Mica. He thinks he knows it all, and he said there'd be less traffic. Less traffic my butt. We can't go over fifty miles an hour. I told him to take the interstate. But no. Not this stubborn husband of mine."

Jack interrupted her, "Beth, we're getting close to the hospital."

"Okay, Jack sweetie, you tell my Claire bear that her momma is on the way," Beth rambled.

"And her daddy!" Mica yelled in the background.

Jack glanced over to Claire. She looked pale and dazed, and she continued to stare out the window as they traveled down the interstate. Jack heard Beth speaking to Mica in the background, and he took the opportunity to relay the information to Claire.

"Baybay, your family is on their way. They're on the Natchez Trace."

"Everyone?" Claire asked, never moving her attention from the window.

Jack shrugged his shoulders in an upward motion. "I'm not sure." Jack turned his attention back to his phone conversation. "Beth?" He waited for a response.

"Yes, Love," Beth said.

"Claire wants to know if everyone's coming or just you and Mica?" he asked.

"Now huuunney, you should know after being a part of this family for so long that this family sticks together," she responded, drawing out honey. "Ezra and Francis are in the backseat. I spoke with Gabby a bit ago, and she was leaving a friend's house in Knoxville to meet us at the hospital. Poor Gaby is just a hot mess with worry," Beth said shaking her head. "At this pace, she may beat us there. Are y'all headed to St. Mary's or Nashville Grace Hospital?" she asked.

"We're headed to Grace," he replied.

"Okay darling, I'll plug it into the GPS. You know we don't know our way around downtown."

"Beth, y'all be careful."

"We will. See y'all soon, Jack. Give my baby girl a big hug from her momma. Jack, when y'all know more, please, please let us know."

"Of course. Drive safely."

Jack hung up the phone and glanced over at Claire. "The whole family's coming," he said. Claire remained silent. Devoid of emotion, her eyes looked hollow, and Jack pressed the accelerator harder.

CHAPTER FOUR

HER HEAD SWUNG AGAINST THE SEATBELT as Jack swerved into the emergency room parking lot. He slammed the drive shaft into park, yanked his car door open, and sprinted around the front of the car towards her door. In a swoosh, her door was open, and a soft breeze brushed against her cheeks. Claire squinted as the sun hit her face.

"Claire, come on sweetheart," Jack said extending his hand toward hers.

She grasped his hands and swung her legs around. Her feet hit the ground. As soon as this happened, she knew that the pain had decreased. *Thank you, God,* she thought.

Her legs shook as she stood. She looked back at the seat of the BMW and saw traces of blood contrasting with the tan, leather seat. Forcing herself to be brave, she stepped forward, and an overwhelming doom encircled her heart. With each step, her feet thudded from the right to left foot as though an anchor was tied onto them.

"Jack," Claire said, turning her head to look at him.

He stopped and looked at her. "Yes, Baybay? What is it? Do you want me to carry you?"

"No." She shook her head slightly. "Can you please pray for us and our baby before we go in there?" she asked, pointing toward the emergency room entrance. "Jack, I'm scared. Our tiny baby." She began to cry again.

He took both of her hands. "Oh BayBay, please don't cry." Jack's heart broke seeing Claire look so helpless. He bowed his head, "Dear Heavenly Father, You know our need now, and I come to You to lift our baby and Claire up to you. You have blessed us with this child, and I know that Your plan was intact long before we became a family. I pray that You will overcome the anxiety and fears surrounding us. I ask that You put a shield of protection over Claire, our baby, and myself. Give us strength to endure and conquer whatever obstacles are heading our way. Amen." He leaned down toward her and kissed her gently on her wet cheek. "Claire, I love you."

Claire looked into his eyes. "I love you too, Jack."

Only a few minutes after entering the emergency room, a nurse escorted them into the first room on the right side of the long, busy hallway. "Claire, my name is Reese, and I'm going to be your nurse today." Claire nodded and followed Nurse Reese to the exam room down the hall. Once they were inside, she turned toward Claire. "How are you feeling?

Claire licked her lips to make them moist. In that instance, Claire realized she was thirsty. "May I have some water, please?" Claire asked hoarsely.

"Of course." Nurse Reese shook her head and extended the blue paper gown "Please undress and put this gown on." Claire's hands shook as she took the gown from her. "Make sure it ties in the front. There is a white bag sitting on the counter for your clothes." Reese smiled kindly at Claire. "I'll go get that water for you."

Claire nodded as she moved the gown closer to her body and hugged it tightly. Hesitantly Claire asked, "Do I need to remove my undergarments?"

Reese recognized the anxiety in Claire's eyes. She had been a nurse in the emergency room for five years. "Yes." She nodded gently. "Hey. Take some deep breaths. It will help; I promise."

Claire breathed in through her nose and out through her mouth. Her chest rose as she breathed in, and her eyes shut as she exhaled. She could feel her pulse racing, and she felt lightheaded as her heart rushed with fear.

"That's it. I want you to work on your breathing while I go get your water and while you change into the gown. Doctor Rodriguez, the attending physician, will be in shortly to examine you." Reese smiled with white, straight teeth, showing no imperfections.

After Reese had exited, Claire did as she was instructed. She changed into the paper gown and climbed onto the table. She inhaled gently and exhaled as she closed her eyes. Her heart seemed to slow with the deep-breathing exercise. She looked between her legs onto the table and noticed that the spotting had subsided. This filled Claire with some comfort of hope.

The room was cold, and the hospital gown did little for comfort. Her body shivered involuntarily.

After what seemed like an eternity, the doctor knocked on the door and entered the room alongside Nurse Reese, who walked toward Claire and gave her a small cup of water. Claire drank, but her eyes never left the doctor.

"Mr. and Mrs. St. John, I'm Doctor Rodriquez." He extended his hand to Jack.

"Hello," Jack said.

Doctor Rodriquez turned his attention to Claire. "Hi, Mrs. St. John." He smiled gently.

"Hi," she said.

"I understand you're twelve weeks pregnant." He moved to sit on the stool.

""Yes, that's correct," she responded.

He nodded, "How many pregnancies have you had?

It's my first pregnancy," Claire said.

Again, he nodded his head and wrote a note into her chart. "When was your last appointment with your obstetrician?"

Claire put her hand to her brow and squeezed her eyebrows toward the center. "It was at eight weeks. Everything was normal during the examination. I . . . I . . . I had an ultrasound at six weeks to check for viability. The ultrasound showed a healthy baby and a strong heartbeat. The heartbeat was one-sixty-five," Claire rambled.

She looked over to Jack for confirmation. Jack nodded and reached toward her hand, taking it. He brought her small hand to his lips and pressed a feather-like kiss upon it.

"My next appointment is this Thurs . . . Thurs . . . Thursday," she slightly stuttered.

"Thank you for the information." He stood from the stool and walked to the sink. He turned the silver handle with one hand while pushing the soap container with the other. "Mrs. St. John, tell me about the symptoms you've been experiencing this morning. And tell me when they began." He reached for a paper towel and dried his hands.

Claire looked at Nurse Reese. "Keep taking those deep breaths. Breath in and out." She smiled and nodded, encouraging Claire to speak.

Claire inhaled deeply. Her body shivered again as the cold moved through her body. Her lips quivered as her teeth chattered. "When I was getting ready for Church, I had some twinges and pains in my lower abdomen. It increased with intensity during Church services, and then I began to spot with blood." She looked at her fingers. Jack squeezed them for support. She looked up at Jack and tried to smile.

"Doctor, does that sound normal for a first pregnancy? Jack asked hopefully.

"Mr. St. John, every pregnancy is different. It's hard for me to know what's normal and what's happening until I examine your wife." He turned his attention to Claire. "Claire, can you go ahead and lay back?"

Claire nodded as she rested her head on the pillow.

Doctor Rod held his gloves in one hand and pulled out the stirrups "I'll be performing a short examination of your cervix. After that, you'll receive an ultrasound to check the heartbeat of the baby, and we'll need to draw blood to do some tests. Do you have any questions for me?" the doctor asked as he put on his examination gloves.

Claire shook her head side. Jack held her hands tightly and squeezed them as the examination began.

"Mr. St. John, do you have any questions?" he asked looking toward Jack.

"No sir," Jack answered.

Doctor Rodriguez turned his attention back to Claire. "Go ahead and rest your head on the pillow. Mrs. St. John, I need you to put your feet in the stirrups and scoot down for me."

As Claire placed her feet into the steel stirrups, a rush of cold air breached her inner parts. She took a deep breath as she squeezed her eyes shut. *How could this be happening? Why is this happening?* she thought.

She felt his hand enter her, and the pressure hurt, as her cervix was sensitive. She readjusted her lower body to find a level of comfort.

The room was silent except for the machines running as he conducted his exam. He placed one hand on her abdomen and pushed gently down.

After a few minutes, he gently slid his hand from Claire. She heard the gloves make a sound as he took them off. Claire slowly opened her eyes for the first time since the exam began.

CHAPTER FIVE

"MRS. ST. JOHN," HE SAID AS THREW HIS examination gloves into the small wastebasket next to him. "You can sit up now." He stood and moved to the sink where he washed his hands.

Claire sat up slowly and huddled her knees closer to warm her body. Claire looked at Jack and saw the puzzlement on his face. She felt tears begin to fill her eyes again.

"Dr. Rodriquez, is everything okay?" Jack asked hesitantly.

Claire looked toward Doctor Rodriguez.

He turned from the sink and leaned against the cabinet. He glanced toward Nurse Reese, and their eyes locked.

"Doctor?" Jack asked again.

He turned his attention to Jack and then to Claire. He swallowed and cleared his throat. "Mr. and Mrs. St. John, there is no easy way for me to say this."

Claire squeezed Jack's hand. Jack placed his second hand on top and covered her hands with his.

Doctor Rodriguez spoke, "After completing an examination of your cervix, I can tell you that your cervix has started to dilate," he stated in a matter-of-fact tone.

Confusion filled Jack's mind. "Doctor, I don't think we understand."

"When a woman becomes pregnant, her cervix closes. In a healthy pregnancy, a women's cervix should be closed until the third trimester." He looked for understanding. "Your wife's cervix is no longer closed. It is open. Unfortunately, this is not normal for a twelfth-week pregnancy.

"Is there a way to close the cervix?" Jack asked.

Doctor Rodriguez paused for a moment. "I'm truly sorry, but it appears you are most likely having a miscarriage," Doctor Rodriguez responded.

A scream pierced the room. "No!" Claire covered her face.

"I'm very sorry." Doctor Rodriguez looked to Jack before continuing, "Before we can confirm that it's a miscarriage, we need to have the ultrasound done. I'll give you both a few minutes, and then we'll bring in the ultrasound machine and draw blood." He waited a moment and then turned to exit the room.

Jack leaned down on the bed and sobbed. Between their shared sobs, the silence between her and Jack was palpable, and Claire knew in her heart that their baby was gone.

After a few minutes, Nurse Reese and two women in scrubs entered the room, pushing an ultrasound cart. Jack raised his head as they entered.

Reese noticed his eyes were red and swollen. "Mr. St. John, I'll have to ask you to move so we can get on that side of the bed," she said softly.

Jack motionlessly took three steps away from the bed to make room for them. Claire looked to Jack for help, and his heart ached.

"Mrs. St. John, it's time for the ultrasound," Reese said.

Claire nodded.

The medical team prepped Claire for the ultrasound by uncovering her abdomen and applying the cold gel. Claire's reflexes responded as the coldness hit her abdomen.

She looked at the ultrasound technician. "Will you turn the monitor toward us?"

She nodded gently. "Sure. We're looking to see if your embryo has a heartbeat along with the position of the embryo."

Claire interrupted. "*Baby*, you mean *baby*. My baby is more than an embryo." Claire began to cry again.

The tech nodded and turned the machine on.

Dr. Rodriguez entered the room, and the team began the ultrasound procedure. Claire and Jack held hands as the sonographer moved the probe up and down on her stomach. Jack squeezed Claire's hand and looked at the screen.

The sonographer exchanged glances with the doctor and shook her head from side to side quickly. Claire saw the silent communication.

"Mrs. St. John, we're going to change the probe and do an intravaginal ultrasound now," Doctor Rodriguez stated.

"Why? Can you not find my baby?" Claire asked, her voice rising in panic.

"A vaginal sonogram will let us see better, okay?" he said gently.

Claire hesitantly nodded.

"This will be a little uncomfortable and cold to the touch," Dr. Rodriguez said.

The sonographer handed him the probe, and he slid it into Claire's vagina. As the intrusion happened, she turned her attention back to the monitor. Then, within minutes, the probe slowly exited her vagina, and the doctor scooted his chair back. Again, he took his gloves off and threw them into the trash.

"Mrs. St. John," he said looking into her blue eyes. He turned his attention to Jack and back to Claire. "I'm truly sorry for your loss. Unfortunately, the baby does not have a fetal heartbeat."

The world grew silent, and despair took over Claire's body.

She could see the doctor's lips moving, but she couldn't make out his words. She looked to Jack, who seemed to be processing the information.

Feeling dizzy, Claire held up her hand. "I think I'm going to be sick."

Nurse Reese hurried to her side and handed her a pan. Jack grabbed her hair and held it as she vomited. Then she dry-heaved and cried with each available breath.

What is happening? How is this happening? Claire thought again as she motioned that she was finished. The nurse handed her a cup of water, and she drank it slowly.

Reese took the cup from Claire and handed her a semi-wet towel. "Here, this should help."

Hoarsely, Claire spoke, "Thanks."

Jack brushed her hair back. "Sweetie, are you okay?"

She only nodded because she felt the wave of nausea begin to rise again. If she spoke, Claire was afraid the vomiting would return.

Doctor Rodriguez waited as Claire cleansed her lips with a towel. "Mrs. St. John, I know this is difficult for you to hear. I'm truly sorry for your loss. However, I need to conduct a D& C, which is a dilation and curettage procedure," Dr. Rodriguez said quietly.

Claire looked to Jack in a panic. "Why? Why do I need that?

Doctor Rodriguez moved closer. "It's to make sure there is no placenta left attached to the uterine wall. If any placenta remains, then the likelihood of an infection or heavy bleeding may occur. We don't want to take a chance on any infection," he said gently.

"Will she have any pain from the D&C?" Jack asked him.

"There should be minimal pain associated with the procedure, but we must remove the contents within the uterine."

He continued, but Claire was too distraught to listen. She squeezed Jack's hand and closed her eyes as tightly as they would shut.

This is just a bad dream, she thought. *Just maybe . . .* and then, the world went dark.

CHAPTER SIX

CLAIRE OPENED HER EYES AND SAW NURSE Reese standing beside her bed. She glanced around the room to orient herself. She saw Jack seated in the blue chair next to the sink. His eyes were swollen and red. Her vision followed the counter to the door, and she did not see the doctor.

"Hey BayBay, you feel asleep," Jack said softly interrupting her stares.

"Asleep?" Claire responded confused. "What time is it?"

"It's a little after three PM," he said glancing at his watch. "We've been here a few hours now."

Still confused, she asked, "Are you sure I fell asleep?"

"That's normal." Nurse Reese spoke softly. She was holding an IV bag in one hand and tubing in the other.

"What's happening?" she asked nervously.

"To perform the D& C, we need to administer some pain medicine. We do have a nurse anesthetist coming in shortly as well," Nurse Reese said.

Tears began again as Claire nodded. "My baby is gone?" Claire asked, hoping that she had been dreaming.

"Yes. I'm sorry," Nurse Reese said with empathy.

Claire lowered her head back onto the pillow and let the tears flow. She thought her body was numb from pain, but she felt a small prick as the needle broke the skin. Claire grimaced.

"I'm sorry if that hurt. The IV is in now, and you should be able to rest comfortably. Do you need anything while we wait on Doctor Rodriguez and the nurse anesthetist?" Nurse Reese asked.

Shaking her head, she muttered, "No. Thank you." Claire turned her attention to Jack. "Are my parents here?"

"I can check. I know Macy and David are in the waiting room. Would you like to see them?"

Claire nodded her head in affirmation.

"I'll go and get them." He walked to her and leaned down. "Claire, I love you." His eyes held hers for a moment.

Claire stared at her husband. She could see pain swirling within his green eyes. "Jack, I'm sorry I couldn't keep our baby safe."

Jack blinked back the surprise of her statement. "Hush that talk, Claire. Don't ever say something like that again. We both know it wasn't our fault." He gently leaned in and brushed his lips to hers.

Claire felt his moist lips touch hers. She was not able to reciprocate his kiss.

He stood back up and gently let her hand go. "I'll go find our family."

Claire nodded and watched as Jack left the room. Alone in the hospital room, her mind raced with the day's events. She felt emotions raging through her body: sadness, emptiness, hurt—and the most powerful of all . . . anger.

She closed her eyes and called out, "Jesus? Are you here? Are you with me?" Anger filled her voice as she lifted her hands toward the ceiling. "Why did you let this happen to me? WHY!"

She clenched her fist so tightly with anger that her knuckles went white. Surprised by the anger, she opened her eyes and inhaled deeply. Relief filled her when she noticed that the room was empty.

Covering her face with her hand she pushed her palm into her eyes. "I just don't understand this. Why? Why my baby?" Tears fell from her covered eyes. "Where are You when I need You most? My heart hurts so much. Please help me understand why this happened to me! Why did You let this happen!"

She sobbed uncontrollably.

"Claire, my child."

The male voice startled Claire, and goosebumps crept up her arms. She sat straight into the bed. "What?" She looked around the room. She saw nothing. "Is someone here?" Confused, Claire stared at the door. "Jack?"

"Claire, I am here. I love you, my child." The male voice spoke. *"I have never left you, and your child is my child."*

The voice. Whose voice was that? Claire didn't recognize it. The anger building within her subsided momentarily. "Who are you?" Claire asked in a whisper.

"I am your loving father, Claire," the male responded.

Claire shifted uncomfortably. *Am I losing my mind?* Familiar voices echoed then, and she saw her family entering the hospital room. *Great. The pain medicine is making me hear voices,* she thought.

"Claire?" Beth's voice was somber as she entered the room.

"Mom." Claire held out her arms toward her mother.

Beth hurried to the bed and embraced her daughter. "Oh, my sweet Claire. Momma's here. Don't you worry; momma's here." The women embraced and cried.

"Claire, how are you holding up?" Mica asked gently walking close.

"Oh, Daddy. I'm not sure," she said, her lips quivering. "Where are Francis and Ezra?"

He patted her hand "They're in the waiting area."

Claire shifted in the bed as Macy came forward. "Macy. David. Thank you for being here," Claire said.

"Always," Macy said with a gentle smile. "I love you. You know, that right?"

"Yes," Claire responded.

"Claire, would you like to pray together?" David asked.

Claire shook her head. As she bowed her head, everyone in the room followed.

"Dear Lord, we come to you with a special prayer request. We ask that you provide peace and comfort over Claire, Jack, and their family as they face this challenge in their life. We lift up Claire and ask that you guide the physician's hands during the next steps. In your name, Amen," David said.

Claire looked at her family and her friends. Each one showed pain. Claire knew they were sad for her, but she also knew they had no idea what she was going through. A heavy feeling weighed on her heart, and she hoped the prayer would bring comfort to her soul because in this moment, she felt no comfort.

"Mrs. St. John, it's time," Doctor Rodriguez said as he entered the room with the nurse anesthetist.

She nodded.

"Doctor Rodriguez, this is my in-laws, Dr. and Mrs. Kline," Jack said motioning toward his in-laws.

"Nice to meet you both." Doctor Rodriguez extended his hand to Mica.

"You as well." Mica shook his hand firmly.

Beth nodded.

"What type of medicine do you practice, Dr. Kline?" Doctor Rodriguez asked.

"Family practice. I own a small clinic back in our hometown," Mica responded.

Doctor Rodriguez nodded in acknowledgment. "Where is home?"

"Hope Valley, Mississippi. Small town just south of the Tennessee line." Mica turned his attention to Claire. "Do me a favor and take special care of my little girl."

"Of course," Dr. Rodriguez said as he turned his attention to Claire. "Any questions for me?"

Claire glanced to her mother. She inhaled a deep breath as the tears filled her eyes again. She inhaled deeply as Beth squeezed her hand. Tears streamed down Claire's cheek. "No sir," Claire said softly.

"I love you, sweetheart," Beth whispered.

Claire only shook her head.

"Me too," Mica stated.

Jack leaned down and pressed his lips to Claire's. "I'll be right here waiting on you. I love you so much, Claire."

"I love you too," Claire said as a nurse rolled her out of the room.

She took one look back as they descended down the hall. Her husband stood beside her parents in tears. Claire's heart ached at the site of her family. She mouthed, *I Love You, always.*

CHAPTER SEVEN

JACK OPENED THE FRONT DOOR TO THEIR home, and the smells of fried chicken filled the air. Claire instantaneously gagged and hesitated to enter. He grabbed her hand and gently nudged her in a forward motion through the doorway. He yelled, "Hello, we're home."

Their heads turned toward the direction of feet treading on the floor. Near the kitchen door, Beth, Mica, Gabby, Ezra, and Francis Kline all scrambled to the mud room entry. Uncertainty clouded their faces, and as soon as Claire met her mother's eyes, she felt like a child again, breaking into sobs. Mica shook Jack's hand and half hugged him as the twins, Ezra and Francis, hung next to the wall awkwardly.

"Shh now, sweetheart. You're home." Beth hurried toward Claire. Beth opened her arms. "Come here, sweetheart. Momma's got you."

Claire let her shoulders slump into her mother's open arms and buried her face.

"Claire, honey, everything's going to be alright," Beth said as she stroked Claire's hair.

Claire silently counted as she took five deep breaths to gain her composure. "Momma, why? Why my baby, momma?"

"Shhh, baby girl. Only Jesus knows why it was time for your sugar baby," Beth said.

"It's not fair momma. Why momma? My baby is gone. Why did Jesus have to take my baby?" She cried harder.

"Come on, shugs. Let's get you to bed so you can get some rest." Beth took her hand while Gabby flanked her left side. The Kline women walked as a unit toward the master bedroom. Looking back toward Jack, Beth said, "Honey, did they prescribe her something to help her rest?"

"Um." Jack exhaled a deep breath. His eyes were weary. "Yes, I need to go to the pharmacy to pick the prescription up."

"We can do it," the twins said simultaneously.

Jack looked over to the boys and nodded. "Thanks, boys. I'm exhausted, so that would be helpful." Jack dug the keys out of his pocket and handed them to one of the twins. "Be careful, please."

The twin nodded and then motioned for his brother to follow. "Sweet! The beamer."

"Boys, make sure you don't speed," Mica said with his eyebrows scrunching sternly.

The boys looked at each other and rolled their eyes at their father.

"I saw that," Mica gruffed. "Teenagers know everything," Mica said to Jack.

Jack forced a small smile and walked toward his office, while Mica made his way down the hallway to the master bedroom.

Mica stood there a moment before gently knocking on the bedroom door.

"Come in," his wife said.

As he entered the bedroom, he took in the surroundings. All three of his girls were situated on the bed. Beth sat with one leg tucked under her. She softly patted Claire's hand while Gabby, his middle child, lay beside her sister.

His heart swelled with love, seeing the women he loved so much. His eyes locked on Beth's green eyes, and her fiery red hair framed her face. After 36 years of marriage, he still loved her as much as the day he first saw her. She smiled at him, and he thought, *I love you.*

Mica's gaze then shifted to his daughters. Gabby and Claire were beautiful, petite girls who favored their mother with their green eyes and light complexion. Gabby inherited her mother's red hair, but she was an introvert, where Beth was extroverted. Claire's hair was like his, a sandy blonde color, and her green eyes sparkled with her complexion. He thought Claire was a mixture of both her parents in personality.

Mica had always thought of Claire as a chameleon with a natural ability to adapt to any situation, and she always seemed to come out on top. But now, he had never seen her so distraught. His heart ached for her, and then suddenly, that ache turned to anger. He closed his eyes tightly and inhaled deeply to let the rush of anger flow through him.

He slowly opened his eyes when he heard his wife softly singing a hymn.

His gaze shifted back toward his Claire bear. There she was—his first born tucked into the bed surrounded by a mountain of pillows. She looked so small to him in that big bed.

He moved to the side of the bed and twisted

awkwardly around Beth to kiss Claire's forehead. "You're strong, my Claire bear. Momma and I will be by your side as long as you need us."

Claire made no effort to answer him as she lay on the bed lifeless. Her mind swirled with uncertainty. *Jesus, why my baby? Why us? How could you take my baby?*

Surrounded by her family, she cried herself to sleep.

Mica, Beth, and Gabby exited the room quietly. They followed the narrow hall to the living room where Jack sat on the couch. He looked defeated. He had his feet propped up on the coffee table, and he was gazing toward the patio door.

"Jack, do you mind if we sit for a bit?" Beth asked.

Without turning his attention toward them, he replied, "Of course not."

Gabby and Beth took seats on either side of him, and Mica sat in the recliner across from him.

Beth extended her arm around Jack, and he embraced his mother-in-law. He couldn't control the emotions he was feeling. His heart was hurting for his wife and their child. The tears streamed down his face. "Shhhhhh. Now, now there, Jack; let it out. It's okay, love," Beth said gently as she patted his back. Beth turned toward her daughter, "Gabby, honey, get us a glass of sweet tea please."

Gabby nodded and left the room.

"Jack, has anyone called your parents?" Mica asked.

Jack inhaled and raised his head. He wiped tears from his face. "No sir. I didn't have time with everything that was happening." Jack paused in the realization he hadn't spoken to his mother. "Oh, Lord help me. My mom is going to die." Jack scratched his forehead.

"Son, do you think it is too late to call?

"What time is it again?" Jack asked, confused.

"Honey, it's after nine PM," Beth said.

"No, they should still be up," Jack replied with a sigh.

"Jack, hand me your phone, and I'll give your dad a call." Mica rose.

Jack punched in his phone code and handed it to Mica. Mica left the room.

"Beth, do you think she'll be okay?" Jack looked to Beth.

"Oh, Jack. My sweet Claire is tough. You know that."

"She loved this baby so much." He looked at his hands. "Did you know we had just picked out a name?"

Beth shook her head. "No, sweetie. She hadn't told me yet."

He inhaled deeply, "We were going to surprise everyone after our next sonogram."

Beth squeezed Jack harder. "Oh honey, it's going to be alright. Don't you worry now. Y'all are both young, and y'all will have plenty of babies."

"I just . . . I just don't know how to help her," he said.

"Honey, I'm not sure if you can help beyond being supportive. Claire will need to emotionally heal from this loss. A momma's loss is like no others, Jack. And we all deal with it differently." Beth paused debating if she should ask. "Jack, what was the baby's name going to be?"

Jack hesitated to answer. "If it was a boy, we were going to name him Landon Jackson."

"Ooh that's such a wonderful name, Jack," Beth cooed. "And if it was a girl?"

He took a deep breath. "Claire loved the name Rose. She wanted to name the baby Landry Rose."

Beth put her hand to cover her mouth. "Oh, Jack. Just beautiful." Beth glanced up as Mica re-entered the room.

He cleared his throat. "Beth, you okay?"

"Yes. We were talking about the baby."

Mica nodded. "Jack, son. Your parents will leave in the morning to head this way. They asked me to tell you that they'll stay a few nights."

"Okay. Thanks." He paused and investigated his folded hands. "I don't know how long it will take for things to be back to normal," he said, not looking up.

"Jack, it'll take time. No matter how long it takes for life to seem normal again, just know you and Claire have so much family that loves you, and we're all here to help y'all," Beth said as she held her hand out and took the sweet tea from Gabby.

CHAPTER EIGHT

"WHO WANTS A HAMBURGER?" JACK CALLED from the grill with his spatula raised high.

"We do!" yelled the twins from the pool.

"Beth and I would like one, please sir," Mica replied from the red hammock situated in the corner under the pergola. He and Beth were lying feet to head, soaking up the glorious sunrays in their swim attire. They each wore sunglasses and held a book in hand.

Thankfully, this Memorial Day had brought about a soft breeze along with the ninety-five-degree sunshine. The soft, east winds broke up some of the thick humidity.

Jack pointed his spatula at the twins. "How many, boys?"

"Two for me," they said in unison. They looked at one another with a smirk and exchanged a high-five.

Jack turned to David. "What about y'all?"

"Six for us would be great." He held up his fingers and counted to confirm. "The kids will eat one, I'll have two, and Macy'll eat one."

"Alrighty then, six for y'all," Jack confirmed. David took a sip of his lemonade as Jack turned his attention back to the grill. "Twelve hamburgers cooked rare coming up," he said with a laugh.

"Rare? Come on, man. Gross," Francis said.

Ezra splashed Francis with water, hitting him directly in the nostrils and eyes. Francis yelled at his brother, and they both lost interest in Jack.

The grill sizzled as Jack flipped the burgers. David stood beside him, assisting, but he was mostly just drinking his lemonade.

Jack and David complemented one another. Being an attorney, Jack liked hard facts, and David understood this about him. He often taught and mentored Jack through a factual route, delivering the scripture in a realistic presentation that revealed the spiritual intent. David had the unique ability to break down scripture and apply it to daily living. Jack believed that David and Macy were a Godsend to their life, and Jack was amazed at the comfort of their friendship.

"So how is Claire doing? How are *you* doing?" David asked.

Jack turned his attention to David. "I'm doing okay, I guess. She's another story, though." He took a deep breath before continuing. "I swear it seems like she cries every day. She won't talk about the miscarriage with me, and when I try to broach the topic of possibly having another baby, she mentally shuts down."

"Jack, everyone grieves in their own way," David said.

Jack nodded. "I get that, I . . . um . . . I just want my wife back—the one who laughed and danced around the house to cheesy nineties music—the wife who quotes scripture when I'm having a bad day." Jack shook his head. "I want the wife who came into my office and teased me into joining her in the bedroom." He sighed. "It's been two months. And you know, she hasn't even been to church since the miscarriage. I don't know what to do."

David shook his head gently in acknowledgment. "Yeah, I know. Macy said the women's bible study hasn't been the same without Claire, either."

"She hasn't even picked up her Bible, and she's short-tempered. She seems angry all the time." Desperation clouded Jack's voice as he flipped the burgers.

David looked over to the round table where Claire and Macy sat. Even from this distance, he could see the sadness on Claire's face. He and Macy had prayed for their best friends daily and tried to be a faithful support system.

"I know this isn't easy, nor have Macy and I had to experience this, but as your pastor and friend, I want to remind you of something. Proverbs 3:5-6 says, 'Trust in the Lord with all your heart and lean not on your own understanding; in all your ways submit to Him, and He will make your paths straight.' Jack, you and Claire won't make it through this without your faith. Anger is a normal process in grief, but with God's mercy and grace, your hearts and minds will be healed. Give her some time and keep faithful during this trying time."

"David, I know God's timing isn't always our timing. I know God's plan is not always known to us, but wouldn't a little insight be wonderful on some occasions?" He flipped another burger. "It's just frustrating. You know how tough it was for us to get pregnant. With all the scheduled ovulation appointments and stuff, we went through a rough period in our marriage. Then, when we gave up the fight, we learned to enjoy each other again, and boom. We got pregnant. Now, here we are. I just wish things would go back to the way things were before the miscarriage. I feel like we're back at square one, in the same place we were years ago," Jack said.

"I think many of us feel that way on occasion, but I guarantee you're better off being patient," David replied wholeheartedly.

Jack looked at his friend and pastor. "You know I haven't lost my faith, right?

David nodded.

"But I *have* lost my wife—or the wife she once was."

David stayed silent for a moment thinking of what to say next. He wanted to be a counselor to his friend and provide him with wisdom. "Man, I wish I could help you both."

Jack shrugged. "I'm trying to not get frustrated, but it's time she lets the anger and sadness go. It's time she gets back into sex with her husband."

"So, we're going there." David laughed.

"Seriously David, you're my best friend. Who else should I talk to about it?"

David nodded. "Good point." He took a sip of his drink. "So y'all aren't having sex?"

"Nope." Jack flipped a burger with strength. "Not regularly. And when we do, she just lays there. It's like she doesn't care about our physical relationship any longer."

"I can't imagine what you're feeling. Have you thought about getting her in to see a grief counselor?" he asked.

Jack looked at David like he was insane. "Seriously?"

David nodded and drank from his drink. "Yes, seriously." He laughed gently.

"Why would I do that? Claire doesn't need a shrink."

"Good grief, Jack. It's not a shrink. It's just someone who can help her sort out her feelings." David laughed.

Jack flipped another burger and shrugged. "I don't know. If something doesn't give soon, I may lose my mind and need a shrink myself." He laughed. "I can't live like this forever. I want my wife back and our normal life back."

"Jack, this isn't your forever situation. It's a trial, and Jesus is testing you," David said.

Jack nodded and breathed deeply. "I hear you, David. I really do. I'm just struggling."

CHAPTER NINE

JACK LOOKED AT CLAIRE SITTING IN HER yellow sunsuit. She had her hair piled into a wild bun, and in true southern fashion, she wore lip-gloss.

God, I love her, he thought. Suddenly, his heart skipped a beat *Did she just smile?* He stared intently to decide if his mind was playing tricks on him. Again, a small smile appeared on Claire's face. *Oh, BayBay, smile some more.* He took a long breath as a feeling of warmth rushed through his blood.

Claire felt Jack's eyes on her, and she turned her head toward the grill. Her eyes locked onto him, and she saw his love for her all over his face. For the first time in two months, she felt a longing for her husband and their relationship. She smiled gently at him and could see the shock resonate on his face.

For the past two months, she had been so involved in her sorrow, she hadn't paid attention to her husband. *What has happened to my life?* Claire thought as she closed her eyes and took several deep breaths. *Jesus, please take the wheel. I don't want to hurt anymore. I want to be normal again. Please, please, Jesus, just take the pain and suffering away."*

"Claire? Earth to Claire. Yoo-hoo." Macy eyed her, wondering what had taken her mind so far away.

Claire opened her eyes and looked at her best friend. "I'm here. I just needed a moment."

"Totally understandable. I need those often myself," Macy said with a smile.

"Do you ever feel like you're sinking?" Claire asked.

"Of course, Claire. What Christian doesn't? What *woman* doesn't? What *mother* doesn't?" She saw a slight grimace cross Claire's face. "Oh, Claire," Macy said, trailing off in shame. "I'm sorry, I shouldn't have said anything about being a mother. How unthoughtful of me."

"It's okay. I know it's hard to be around me right now. I don't expect you to walk on eggshells." She took a sip of her sweet tea. She looked back at Jack. He and David were in a deep conversation. "Look at those two." She pointed toward them to change the conversation. Macy turned her chair around to get a better look. "What do you think they're talking about?" Claire asked.

Macy let out a soft chuckle. "You, honey. Haven't you seen the way Jack keeps eyeing you?"

She laughed gently. "Will life ever be normal again? Will I ever be me again, Macy?"

"Whose life is normal?" Macy chuckled. "Lord help me, I don't think life is normal for anyone, Claire." Suddenly, Macy whipped her head around. "You better not let me see you run again, missy!" Macy yelled at her oldest daughter, Emma. "Sorry, Hun," she said turning her attention back to Claire. "Those kids of mine will make my hair go grey sooner than I need it to." Macy saw the lonely gaze in Claire's expression, and her heart ached for her dearest friend.

Claire smiled gently and shrugged her shoulders. She looked toward the pool and saw Emma cautiously climb into the pool. She saw Emma's eyes widen as the coolness of the pool overtook her breath. Claire's heart filled with envy, and jealousy crept into her body. "You're so lucky," she blurted out unintentionally.

Macy trod lightly, noticing Claire's tone shift. "Claire, how are you? I mean, really, how are you? What's going on up here?" Macy asked pointing to her head.

"Honestly?"

"Yes, honestly," Macy responded. "You know I'm here for you."

She shrugged her shoulders. "I had life planned out. I knew where I wanted to go to college. I knew which major I would pick. I knew which career I wanted. I knew I would marry Jack when we met. I knew where we would live. I knew I would be a mother someday. I had every chapter of my life planned out."

Macy watched her friend. "We both know life isn't ours completely to plan."

Claire held air into her mouth and then exhaled it. "I know that," she said with a hint of aggravation. "But how did it derail so quickly? I don't have a plan. What do I do without a plan?"

"Claire, listen to me. As humans, we feel like we're the drivers of our life. And when we wreck, we feel like we lose control. But honey, you know better than any other woman I know—our life is not our own. Our life is what God has planned for us, and sometimes that includes trials that test our faith and love. And that is what is happening to you—a trial of your obedience, love, and faith. For God and your marriage. You have to let go of the hurt and fight to find the path that God is directing you toward."

Claire studied her friend. Macy was an amazing friend who loved God with all her heart, but Claire didn't want to hear that God had a plan. *How could God's plan involve my baby dying?* she thought.

"Well, it's easy for you to say that," Claire snapped. "You've never lost a child, and it was easy for you to get pregnant. too. You have no idea what I'm going through."

Macy's eyes widened. "You're right, Claire. I haven't been through this, but nobody has an easy life. We've all been through trials."

Claire felt guilty for the snippy reply. "I'm sorry, Macy. It's so strange—life after losing a baby. You expect the world to stand still while you grieve. But nope. It doesn't miss a beat, and everything keeps going on like nothing happened. I go to work, to the grocery store, to the gym, and everything seems so normal, and yet, my inside is torn to pieces with anger and sorrow. Then the people I encounter like the doctors I call on, the nurses, my manager, all of them. They smile at me like I'm damaged goods. Everybody's tiptoeing around me, and they don't know what to say. And I guess I get it because here I am snapping at you."

"It's okay, Claire. I completely understand," Macy said.

"It's funny. People try to make small talk with me, or they say in the worse tone ever, 'Bless your heart.' I swear Macy," Claire said with exasperation, "if I hear one more 'Bless your heart,' I may scream. Wouldn't that be something to see? Me losing my mind on people?"

Macy laughed loudly, and Claire looked at her strangely. Macy dropped her head into her hands, and laughter vibrated through her fingers. She looked up at her friend with a semi-serious expression.

"Why are you laughing? I'm being serious, and you're laughing like this is some kind of joke?"

"Honey," Macy said in a doting manner. "You know I'm laughing *with* you, right? I was just picturing you going off on some sweet old lady who said, 'Bless your heart.'" Macy leaned over and patted Claire's hand. "Look, people are awkward, and Jesus knows they put their foot in their mouths more often than not. But Bless *their* hearts, they *are* trying. They say stupid things at the wrong time because the silence makes it more awkward. You have to take it with a grain of salt and see it for what it is—an effort to show they care."

Claire rolled her eyes at Macy. "I get it. I'm just . . . ugh." She moaned and put her hand to her forehead. "But I swear. Seriously, I hate that phrase. I'm not kidding. If I hear one more 'Bless her heart,' I *will* lose my mind."

Macy laughed gently. She took a sip of her tea and wiped the sweat from her upper lip. "Seriously though, Claire. You have to give it to God. With a loss like this, you can't try to get over it on your own."

Claire cleared her throat and closed her eyes. "Macy, no offense, but can we have one single conversation without you bringing up God—or telling me what I *need* to do?"

Unfazed, Macy replied quickly. "Claire, I'm a preacher's wife. It's part of my role, and more importantly, I'm a Christian. I'm just telling you the truth, and I know you might not want to hear it right now, but you can't expect me to not talk about the Lord. The Lord is the center of my life."

"Well, He's not the center of *my* life," Claire snapped.

An awkward silence followed, and Macy took another sip of tea.

"What I meant to say," Claire said, "is that God is not the center of my life *right now*. And as a Christian, I know I'm supposed to lean on Him and trust Him. But you know what? I need a break from that. When we were trying to conceive, I was angry about how difficult it was. Then, when we finally got pregnant, I felt guilty about not trusting the Lord. And then He goes and takes . . ."

"Claire, you can't . . ."

"Stop it, Macy. I mean it. You can't *preach* me into feeling better. It won't work, and I'm tired of talking about it. I'm just asking you, as a friend, to lay off the holy-roly crap around me for a while."

"Well, like I said, Claire, God is part of who I am, so I can't make any promises, but I *will* try to be more mindful of your feelings."

"Thank you. Now, excuse me. I need to go to the restroom."

Still at the grill, Jack saw Macy and Claire in what seemed to be an argument. *They can't be fighting,* Jack thought. *They're best friends.* Then, Claire abruptly stood and marched into the house. *Dang it. And with that smile earlier, I thought today would be a good day for her.*

Sitting alone now, Macy looked toward the pool where her oldest child Emma was still playing. Emma had turned four in January. Lucy was two, and their youngest, Amber, was nine months old. Amber and Lucy were lying down in one of the guest rooms for an early afternoon nap, and you could hear the softness of their breaths through the baby monitor. Macy couldn't imagine losing one of her children. *Poor Claire,* Macy thought. *But I don't know how to help her without talking about the Lord.*

Soon, Claire rejoined Macy, but neither of them said a word. They both watched Emma, who was pulling herself up the side pool ladder. She slowly climbed until she had both feet flat on the concrete. Her smile was bright. "Look mommy—I did it." Emma squealed in excitement as she stood on the edge of the pool.

"Great job, sweetheart. Be careful please," Macy called back. Emma gave her a thumbs up and made her way to the diving rock. Emma climbed onto the diving rock. She looked so tiny against the big rock, and Macy edged closer in her chair with a protective measure. Emma smiled and waved with enthusiasm while looking toward Macy for approval. Macy nodded slightly and waved toward her. "You can do it, baby girl; Momma believes in you," Macy shouted.

Emma nodded and took a step to the edge of the rock. She looked down into the water and froze.

"Go ahead, baby girl. You've got this. Jump," David called from the grill.

Emma waved at David and inhaled a deep breath. A splash engulfed the pool a few feet away from the diving rock, and Emma rose to the top of the water. "Did you see me, momma? Did you see?"

"Yes, honey. You were amazing." Macy blew her daughter a kiss.

Claire saw the love in Macy's eyes for her children. And she felt a familiar sting—the ache of her heart for their child, but then Claire felt another familiar stab in her stomach—jealousy. She cringed as the envy arose.

"Macy?"

"Yes?" Macy turned her attention back to Claire.

"I know it's been a while since I've been to church. And considering what I just said to you, I know you must think I'm terrible." She watched Macy's expressions, anxiously looking for any signs of disapproval.

Macy paused and thought about her answer. "Claire, grief manifests itself in so many different ways. Who am I to judge you? It's not my place. And I know you want me to lay off talking about God, but Claire, I know you're a Christian. And as Christians, we have to hold on to faith when we go through grief."

Claire exhaled a breath of air. "I'm just angry. I have no doubt that God is in control, and I know that He can do anything, but that's why I'm so mad. I don't get it. Why did his plan include my baby dying? God *could* have saved my baby. Macy, you know the struggle we faced to conceive."

Macy nodded.

"Granted, we didn't go through what some couples do, but we tried so hard to have this baby. We prayed and prayed. I read my bible every day, I tithed religiously, and I did everything a faithful and good Christian should do. But what did I get?" She put her sunglasses on to cover the anger in her eyes.

"God doesn't promise us a life without sorrow or pain. You know that more than anyone. But our faith is tested in situations that hurt us the most. You have to fight the devil's urge to make you angry. Grieve, yell, do whatever you need to do, but get back into your faith. God is testing you and Jack, your marriage, your faith, your love. I know you, and you're for love for Jesus is glorious, and I can see the pain you are going through."

Tears welled up in Claire's eyes.

"Claire, look at me," Macy said leaning closer. "Life goes on. I know that sounds harsh, but it's the truth. God created us to be able to move past trying times. He loves us, and thereby, *we* are able to love. I will never . . ."

Claire interrupted her. "Just stop. I shouldn't have brought it back up. I don't want to do this with you, Macy. But it's easy for you to say 'life goes on.' You have three beautiful girls and the family you always wanted." Claire pointed to the pool at Emma as tears streamed down her face. "You're a momma," Claire said, her voice harsh, "and that's all I want to be. I want my child back in my stomach. I want to have the chance for my child to be in the pool playing with your girls. Two years, Macy. Two long years of peeing on pregnancy sticks, watching for the perfect date, laying in the bed for thirty minutes so no sperm would exit. You name it! I did it *all*, just to conceive. And on that Saturday when I took those three pregnancy tests, my life changed. Just like that, those pink lines represented the one thing I had prayed so hard for."

Macy remained silent, her eyes on her daughter.

Claire could feel a building sob waiting to emerge, so she pushed back her lawn chair. "Excuse, me. I need to go freshen up."

Macy grabbed her hand as she passed by. "Claire, I love you, and when God gives you children, you will be an amazing momma. Please, please my darling friend, don't give up on hope."

Claire didn't respond and freed her hand. She made her way to the French doors, which connected the family room to the back-pool area. She felt the coldness from the air conditioner hit her face, which sent a sliver of chills up her arms. She hugged herself to eradicate the chills crawling up her arms.

She went to the brown cow-print couch and sat. As she rested, she tried to remember the last time she had knelt to pray. *Surely it wasn't the day of the miscarriage,* Claire thought and took a deep breath. Guilt slithered up into her throat. *Maybe I should pray.* She shook her head and wiped her tears. *No, I don't have anything to say to you right now, God.*

CHAPTER TEN

THE PATIO DOORS OPENED, AND SHE HEARD footsteps nearing the couch.

"Hey Baybay, there you are. I was wondering where you went off to. The burgers are ready," Jack said, using his pet name for her.

She closed her eyes and thought about the first time he told her he loved her. He was sitting in front of the student union, and he called out, "Hey," as she crossed the entrance. She could still remember the flutters in her stomach as she ran up to him and plastered him with a kiss.

"BayBay, I love you," he had said.

She gazed back into his eyes. "BayBay? Ooh, I love that. Is that my new nickname?"

He looked curiously at her. "You love the nickname? Is that all?"

She grinned mischievously, and then she kissed him again. "Jack Hudson St. John, I love you from the bottom of my feet to the tip-top of my head."

Then, he had grabbed her by the waist and twirled into a circle. In that moment, she knew she would marry him one day.

"Claire? Did you hear me?" Jack asked, snapping her back to the present. She opened her eyes to see her husband smiling and standing over her. He pulled the ottoman closer to her and sat down. "Rest is a good thing on hot days." He smiled.

"I'm sorry I left the fun. I just had to take a break. I was trying to have a good time, Jack." She ran her hands through her hair and blew out a puff of air.

He stroked the pieces of hair that had fallen from her bun.

"I know everyone is expecting me to just snap out of it and enjoy the day. And for the most part, I did. But then Macy started preaching at me, and I can't, for the life of me, keep the anger from rising. I know I've been horrible to handle, and I truly am sorry. I can't . . . I don't know how to describe to you what's happening inside my head; it's like I'm drowning in grief."

"Baybay," he said lovingly. "*God* is your life vest and your anchor. Grab ahold of it and hold on. Claire, I have loved you since the moment we met in college. When we said our vows, I promised to love you for better or worse. God never promised us a life without hurt or a life without trials, and I never assumed it would always be easy. He loves us, Claire, and I know this seems like our absolute worse time as a couple. I pray this is it BayBay, but there are no guarantees, except one. With Jesus by our side, we can survive."

She studied her husband. He was such a wonderful husband, and guilt once again crept up her spine. But immediately, anger took over, and she yelled the first thing that came to her mind. "Jesus, Jack, you too? Why in the hell is everyone preaching to me today? Are y'all trying to make up for me missing so much church? You're my husband. Can't you just be here for me without shoving God down my throat?"

Immediately, Claire saw the pain in his eyes. A pang penetrated her heart, and she felt her grief waging a war against her love for him.

"Claire, I just want you back. I want my wife and my rock back. Please, I'm begging you to fight this anger taking control over you. I need you to come back to me. Come back to *us*." He had tears in his eyes.

"I'm sorry," she said in response. She loved that he loved her so much, and she felt embarrassment slither into her throat. "Jack, I love you." She began to cry. "I don't know how to fight this. It hurts so much. You have no idea what's happening to me, internally. No one does." She sniffed and cleared her throat. "I'm drowning in sorrow, Jack. I'm just drowning."

Jack studied his wife. She looked completely broken. His heart ached for her. Jack leaned down to kiss her lips softly. For the first time in weeks, she responded. He intensified the kiss, and she placed her arms around his neck. She felt a longing rise into her body.

He gently pulled back, and the haze of love shined on his face. "I miss you, Claire. I miss *us*." He extended his hand, and she took it.

"Me too, Jack," she said.

The patio door quickly opened, and a soaking-wet twin entered. "Momma said to tell y'all we're gonna eat all the burgers. Get your butts out here now." The twin ran out, slamming the door on his way out.

Jack groaned and shook his head. "Which one was that?"

"Seriously? That was Ezra," Claire said amused. "You still can't tell my brothers apart?"

"Nope. And I'm not cleaning up the water on the floor either." Jack took her arm into his, and they walked to join the others.

CHAPTER ELEVEN

As he shut the front door, they waved goodbye to everyone except Claire's family.

"What an amazingly fun day," Beth said.

"Here-Here," Mica said while yawning. "I'm tired, sweetheart. Let's head on to bed now."

"Goodnight," Jack called.

"Goodnight," Beth said.

"Goodnight, son," Mica called.

The twins and Gabby were curled up in the living room watching a zombie movie. Gabby had a blanket pulled up to her nose, and the boys were shoving popcorn into their mouths.

"What are y'all watching?" Jack asked the group.

Gabby looked toward Jack without letting the blanket fall. "Zombies Doomsday Bloodbath."

"Seriously, they have a movie named that?" Jack asked, shaking his head.

"Dude, it's the best," Ezra said not moving his eyes from the television.

"Alrighty then." Jack laughed. "Good night, y'all. We'll see you in the morning," he called as he set the alarm and turned down the hall toward their bedroom.

"Goodnight," Ezra, Francis, and Gabby replied.

Jack and the Klines had planned on attending the early church service tomorrow, which began at eight-thirty AM. Then they would spend the rest of the day at the lake. He was excited about taking the boat out on the lake. It would be the first time for the season, and it was one of his and Claire's favorite things to do together.

A surge of hope coursed through his veins as he stood in front of their bedroom door with his hand on the knob—a hope that tonight they would reconnect mentally—and physically. He really hoped that he and Claire would make love like they did before the miscarriage two months ago—that they would succumb to their needs. Most importantly, he hoped that life would get back on track and his best friend would be there again—that their love would conquer, as it had in the past.

Jack opened the door and entered the dimly lit room. He surveyed the area, looking for Claire. He spotted her standing beside the bed in her lingerie. His heart skipped a beat. He walked closer to her and looked into her eyes. "You look amazing."

Claire blushed. "Jack, I miss you."

"Oh Claire, you don't know how much I miss us."

"Will you kiss me now?"

As his eyes twinkled, he leaned into her and kissed her gently. He felt his body react as her moist lips touched his. She placed her hands behind his head, and he moved closer so that no space existed.

Jack backed away and swung his arms under her body to gently pick Claire up. "Ooh." She laughed.

"Oooh la la," he said grinning. "You're all mine." He lowered his head to hers and kissed her passionately,

Claire's body responded. Her pulse quickened as her mouth succumbed to his. She felt Jack situating her on their bed, and she felt his pressure as he situated his body above hers.

"While I have your undivided attention, I want to ask you something." He kissed her ear.

"Ask me something? Now? Seriously, Jack?"

He laughed a deep throaty laugh. "I'm afraid I'll forget."

Claire kissed the side of his neck, and he groaned. "You were saying?"

"That's not fair. But please don't stop." He moaned as his lips played with her lips. He broke free and looked into her eyes, hesitant to ask the question. He kissed her lips and then trailed a kiss down her neck. "So, we are going to Church in the morning as a family." He continued to kiss her neck. "And I really, really want you to go."

As quickly as the words let his mouth, he felt her body stiffen under his. He trailed his kisses back up to her cheek.

"Claire?" he asked.

"Get up," she said with anger.

Jack looked up at her in shock and saw anger in her eyes. "What?"

"Get off me." She saw a flicker of confusion and pain cross his face.

Jack, stunned by her reaction, slowly rose and sat on the side of the bed while she shifted upward in the bed, pulling the cover high to her neck. "Seriously Claire, what is wrong with you?"

"What is wrong with *me*? How could you ask that!" she yelled. "You were literally in the middle of making love to me, and the first thought you had was to ask me if I'd go to church?"

He looked at her, and a flash of anger crossed his face. "I don't know you anymore. I don't know how to fix us."

"Fix *us*? You think you can fix us, Jack? You do realize we lost a child, right? Remember, I had a baby in my stomach." She moved her hands to her stomach. "*Our* baby!" Claire grabbed a pillow and tossed it at him.

His reflexes were quick enough to catch the pillow. "Seriously, Claire. Are you crazy?" he asked, stunned by her behavior.

"Crazy, really? Crazy! I'm not crazy, Jack. I'm angry! Are you oblivious to what is happening in our life?" Her pulse quickened as the anger rushed through her veins. She shook her head in frustration. "Jack, what is wrong with *you*? You seem perfectly fine and normal. You go to work like nothing happened. You don't cry for our child, and you surely don't mourn." She watched him, waiting for a response. Still no response. "Why are *you* okay? Why are you trying to continue like everything is just fine and dandy?"

He put his face in his hands. "Claire, I'm just trying to move on with our life. I want things to be normal again."

Jack turned to look at her, and Claire felt a small amount of guilt creep into her heart. She saw the pain and confusion flickering in his eyes. Softening her tone, she asked, "Why did you think it would be okay to ask me to attend church? Jack, just this afternoon, I told you and everyone to back off."

As Claire's anger subdued, Jack felt his anger increase. "Do you want me to stop trying? Is that it? Have you just given up on everything? Have you seriously given up on your faith, us, everything?"

She waited a moment as confusion stirred in her head. She had gone from happy to angry so quickly. "I don't know, Jack. I just don't know." Claire shook her head as the realization bombarded her emotions. For the first time in her life, Claire was confused about her faith, her love for Jack, and her life.

Jack stood and walked toward the closet. "It's been two months, Claire. Sixty days!" He took a thick black blanket out. He walked to the bed and yanked his pillow from the bed.

"I know how long it has been, Jack. My mind knows, but my heart can't seem to let it go." She moved closer to the edge of the bed. Jack stood holding his pillow in one hand and his blanket in the other. "Where are you going?" she asked.

"To sleep on the couch. I can't do this anymore, Claire." He made no effort to face her as he spoke.

"What do you mean by you can't do this? This as in *us*?"

Jack hesitated to find the words. "Claire, I love you. I'm not trying to give up on us, but I just don't know how to do this anymore. I'm tired of it. I need you to fight for us as much as you're fighting to *not* move forward."

He walked out the door.

CHAPTER TWELVE

"AMAZING GRACE, HOW SWEET THE SOUND that saved a wretch like me."

Claire heard her mother's voice floating through the bedroom. Geez. *I just can't escape the church pressure, can I?* She stretched, smelled the scent of bacon, and then moaned with pleasure.

The sun tried to enter the room as a ray beamed through the satin curtain. She turned to her side and propped her head on her elbow. She was shocked Jack didn't come back to bed. A wave of embarrassment poured over her. She pushed up in the bed and looked at the clock. It was seven AM. She closed her eyes. In her heart, she knew her reaction to Jack's question had been over the top. Regardless of how she felt now, this newfound anger seemed to erupt within her spontaneously and wouldn't allow her to show grace to anyone.

Claire inhaled deeply as last night's scenes replayed in her mind again. She closed her eyes and tried to will away the evening. "A Pillow. How could I throw a pillow at my husband? Who am I now?" She blew out a rush of air.

"My child, hear me. I give Grace as should you."

Stunned by the familiar male voice, Claire looked around the room. "Jack?" No answer came. Claire shook her head in disbelief. This was the second time she had heard the male voice. "Am I going crazy?" she asked herself.

Claire shook off the moment and made her way to the bathroom. She deeply inhaled as the smell of Jack's aftershave filled her nostrils. It must have not been long since he had been there.

As she sat on the toilet, she placed her head into her hands. "What's happening? Things are so out of control." She got up and washed her hands. Claire put on her robe and stood in front of her bedroom door. "You can do this, Claire. It's just your family. Jack loves you," she said to herself.

She went down the hall into the kitchen and saw her mother standing over the stove. She walked behind her and kissed her gently on the cheek. "Hi, Mom. It smells yummy."

"Well, there you are sleepy head," Beth said eyeing her intently.

Mica looked up from the Sunday paper and smiled over his reading glasses "Mornin."

"Good mornin, Daddy," Claire said as she made her way to him. She bent down and kissed the top of his head.

Her eyes lifted, and she saw Jack standing in the butler pantry. He held the coffee pot in one hand and the cup she had given him for his birthday in the other. It read *#1 Dad*. Her heart skipped another beat. Claire slowly made her way toward him. As she approached, she saw that his eyes were puffy and red. She felt a string of love fill her heart. *Oh, Claire, fix this*, she thought. "Jack?" she asked softly.

Jack took his coffee cup and pressed it to his lips. "Claire," he said, not making eye contact.

"Can we talk?"

"About?"

"Jack, please?"

"After breakfast. Your mother has been cooking all morning." He walked toward the table. "Good morning, Mica. Good morning Beth," Jack said, as he pulled up his seat.

Mica eyed Jack and Claire. "Jack, did I happen to see you sleeping on the couch in your office?"

"What?" Beth asked shocked from the kitchen. She leaned her head out to see the table.

Claire looked at her father. "Really, dad?" She walked toward the table.

Jack looked at Claire as she pulled her seat next to his. "Mica, actually, I did sleep in my office."

"What in the world for?" Beth looked toward Claire. "Claire, why did Jack not sleep with you?"

Claire shrugged her shoulders.

"Really, you have no idea?" Jack asked narrowing his eyes at her.

"Not right now, Jack," Claire said, embarrassed. She could see anger on his face. It was the first time she had seen him confrontational in front of her parents.

Mica cleared his throat. "Alright, let me say this to you both. I don't know what happened last night to make you both angry enough to sleep in separate rooms, but I do know that whatever it is needs to be fixed. You two have been together for a long time, and that is not something that can be just thrown away." He looked from Jack to Claire.

"Daddy, we're okay." Claire looked to Jack, but again, he didn't make eye contact.

Beth walked to the table and surveyed each of them. She could feel the tension palpitating the room. Beth looked sheepishly at Claire and asked, "Are you going to church with us this morning, sugar?"

Claire cast a side-ways wary look at Jack. He made no effort to acknowledge her. "No, mama. I'm not going to church. I don't even know if I can *ever* go back to that church again. That's literally the place where I lost my baby."

Mica straightened in his chair. "Claire Bear." Claire turned her attention toward him. "You know a place is not the reason for your pain. God's house is a place of worship and of comfort."

"Daddy, how am I supposed to find comfort in the place where my miscarriage happened? How do I let go of those memories?"

"Through your faith, sweetheart. Our faith gives us peace and comfort. Lean on God, Claire Bear, and you'll find your comfort," Mica responded.

Claire shook her head as the anger rose within her. "Y'all don't understand. I'm not asking you to agree with me, but I *am* asking you to respect my decision." Then she hurried out of the kitchen to the bedroom, and the sound of a slamming door reverberated through the house.

"Well, she has to let the anger out if she's ever gonna let it go," Beth said quietly.

Mica looked over at his son-in-law and saw the disappointment on his face. "Son, it's going to be okay. I know you're worried about her, but she has to find her own way in this. She and her Savior need to spend some time together in conversation."

"Mica, I really *am* trying to be understanding. We had a huge fight last night. It's probably the worst fight we have ever had." He rubbed his hands through his hair. "I know we lost a baby, but we have to move on at some point."

"Moving on will happen. Just don't push her too hard. You and I both know she's a champion of free will, and the more you, her mother, or I push, the harder she'll push back."

Suddenly, Claire walked back into the kitchen, and an awkward hush hovered in the room.

"I'm sorry I got angry," Claire said. "Coffee. I need some coffee." To change the subject, Claire asked, "Where are the boys and Gabby?"

"Well, the hoodlum brothers are still in the bed. It's amazing the amount of sleep those two need," Mica said as he drank a sip of his coffee. "Gabby's running on the treadmill because heaven forbid, she miss a day of exercise. When she comes home for a visit, your momma tries to get her to eat breakfast, but she prefers some type of vegan granola bar. She even brings her bars with her," he said shaking his head. "What in the heck is the purpose of a vegan granola bar?" He lathered his plate with another biscuit and another piece of bacon. "I tell my patients to exercise, stay within portion limits, and eat what you like. Humph. Granola."

"Mica, seriously, as a doctor, one would think you know the benefits of healthy eating. For twenty years, I've warned you about how bacon's not good for your heart. You're gonna just drop dead one day if you don't watch what you eat and start exercising," Beth griped.

"Then don't cook bacon," he said matter-of-factly.

Beth huffed at him and turned her attention back to Claire and Jack. "The new pot of coffee's done, Claire. Grab you a cup, and you and Jack come sit down for some breakfast."

Claire stretched on her tip toes to reach the top shelf. Then, she made her coffee with three sugars and more creamer than coffee.

Beth grabbed two plates and sat them down on the table. "I cooked a big breakfast. Homemade buttermilk biscuits, gravy, bacon, and some scrambled eggs." She winked at them. "I sure do hope y'all are hungry."

"You better eat your share before the boys get up. Cause Good Lord knows, they eat us out of house and home," Mica grumbled.

Jack chuckled. "Mica, they're growing boys."

"Growing boys? Hush yo mouth, Jack. Those two eat probably fifty thousand calories a day. I've never seen two boys put so much food away. When they have football practice, they come home and eat an extra-large pizza."

"That's doesn't sound that bad," Jack said as he grabbed a biscuit.

"Each!" Mica bit into his biscuit and grabbed up a piece of bacon.

Beth eyed her husband as he put the bacon on his plate. "Mica, that's your third piece of bacon."

"Beth, like I said earlier, if you don't want me to eat the bacon, then don't cook the bacon." He winked at her.

She shook her head at her husband and turned her attention to Jack and Claire. "I can't believe they're gonna be seniors this year," Beth said with a pout. "It happens so quickly, doesn't it, Mica?

"Yep. Before you know it, the kids think they're smarter than you, and all they want is money so they can hang out with their friends."

Jack and Claire both giggled at Mica's bluntness. Claire loved her daddy and his stern attitude. He was a hardworking man who had provided a more-than-comfortable home for his family. He had a gentle yet firm spirit that drove her mother crazy most of their marriage.

"All my babies are growing up so fast." Beth caught herself and glanced at Claire. "Oh, honey. I'm sorry."

Claire took a sip of her coffee and cleared her throat. She looked at the trio with determination across her face. "Okay, listen up, everyone. I have an announcement to make. As of today, I don't want anyone in this family to apologize to me again. Say whatever you need to say, but don't feel sorry for me. All I ask is that y'all lay off with the advice. I'm *not* going to church. Quit asking. I know y'all are worried about me, but this is something I have to work through. Am I hurting? Yes. Am I angry? Yes. And yes, I know I'm difficult to deal with. As you can obviously tell, Jack and I had an argument last night." She glanced to Jack. He looked up from his plate. She smiled, and he responded with a half-smile. "But we will be fine."

"Honey, a word of advice. Don't go to bed mad at each other; no argument is worth it," Beth said with her face pinched awkwardly.

Mica chuckled. "Beth, she just said to lay off with the advice, and the first thing you do is give her your 'word of advice.'"

"I'm her momma," Beth said. "I can't stop giving her advice. Besides, it's a good rule. If you're gonna get mad before bed, then you need to make up and have makeup sex before you go to sleep."

Jack spit out his biscuit in a cough.

"Geez, Momma," Claire said.

"Honey, you know I don't hold nothing back," Beth said.

"That's the truth," Ezra responded.

Claire couldn't hold back her giggles, and laughter imploded on Jack's lips, as the weight of last night's argument lifted.

Claire cleared her throat. "I am *not* going to talk about my sex life with my parents over breakfast, but seriously, listen to me, all of you. I'm trying to figure out life and how to manage. I'm tired of being angry, I'm tired of crying, and I'm tired of the hurt. I really just want to feel normal again. So, let's just make this a fun, normal day." She turned to look at her husband. "You and I can talk later if you want, or we can let it go."

Jack looked at her. Claire was the love of his life, and today seemed to make more sense. He still longed for the time before the miscarriage. "Claire, I loved you from the moment I met you. I'll always love you. I do need for us to figure out how to maneuver through this trial. But I don't want to face it without you."

She leaned over and kissed him.

Mica grunted, "We *are* at the table, you two. If y'all wanna makeup like Beth advised, you can head to the bedroom now."

Claire and Jack both laughed. "Oh, Daddy you've seen us kiss before."

"Well, that doesn't mean I need to see it while I'm eating my biscuits and gravy."

"And bacon," Beth said jokingly.

CHAPTER THIRTEEN

SHE HEARD THE GARAGE DOOR OPEN, and Claire knew her family was home from church. The boys barreled in first. "Hey sis," they said in unison as they hurried down the hall.

"Hi there. What's the hurry?" she asked.

"We need to get our swim trunks on," Ezra shouted in a boisterous sprint.

"And we have to make a few phone calls to the ladies back home." Francis winked at his sister.

"Um. Okay, Francis." She rolled her eyes. Gabby came in next, and Claire was stunned by how famously radiant she looked in a green empire waist dress that stopped mid-calf. "Wow, you look amazing, sis."

"Well, gracias, senorita." Gabby winked at her sister with an attitude of grace.

"De nada, bella dama," Claire said spiritedly.

Claire and Gabby learned Spanish in high school. They used it as code when living in their childhood home to keep their parents from listening in on their conversations. Their father could not speak a lick of it, and when they spoke, he would always yell, "Speak English, you two. What are you hiding you don't want us to hear?"

When Claire heard her father yell, "Hey," she knew he was going to give the same lecture he delivered back then. "I heard that. Why in the world can't you just speak English? We live in America, after all." Mica shook his head and headed toward the kitchen. "What'd y'all say anyway?"

Her father's predictability started a giggle that Claire couldn't control. *God, it feels good to laugh,* she thought. When she finally calmed her laughter, she said, "Daddy, I told Gabby she looked beautiful, and she thanked me. That's all."

Beth entered the mudroom with a smile as warm as the yellow dress she wore. "Oh, Mica. Spanish is such a romantic language. If you weren't so pig-headed, maybe you'd learn a little Spanish to add a splash of romance to our life." Beth turned her attention to her daughters. "My beauties. You are both absolutely gorgeous. Oh, how I love you both so much." She kissed each one on the cheek and followed her husband.

"Hola." Jack laughed as he placed his keys down on the mudroom table. He leaned over and kissed his wife.

"Hola, el hombre," Gabby said laughing.

"Would y'all stop that already!" Mica yelled from the kitchen.

All three broke out into laughter. Claire placed her hand over her stomach. "Goodness, I haven't laughed this much in a while. I forgot how aggravated Daddy gets."

"Jack, sometimes Claire and I would speak Spanish the whole time during dinner. He'd get mad as a wet hen," Gabby said.

"Sure did," Claire said. "Remember, Gabby? One time he threatened to take our phones away."

"Oh, yeah. Fun times for sure, sis." Gabby winked.

"Well luckily I know Spanish, or I might worry what you two girls are up to, myself," Jack said with a twinkle in his eye.

When Gabby left them standing alone, Claire took Jack's hand and looked up at him. "Are we okay?"

Jack shrugged his shoulders. "We will be. I don't want to fight with you anymore, Claire. I want to move past the anger."

"Me too. Jack, I'm sorry for how I acted last night."

"You threw a pillow at me," he said, smiling sheepishly.

"True. I did throw a pillow." She winked. "Did it hurt?"

"Hurt? Have you not seen these guns lately?" he asked, pointing to his arms.

"I guess not. Let me feel those big guns." She pressed her fingers into his arms. Arousal fluttered, and she stood on her tip toes to kiss him lightly. Her heart raced.

"Come on, loves. Get in here and make yourselves a sandwich. I'm ready to hit the lake," Beth yelled as she slathered mayonnaise onto two pieces of bread. She placed her tomatoes on top and passed the butter knife to Mica.

She and Jack broke apart and laughed. "Just another day with the Klines," Claire said.

"I wouldn't trade it for the world," he replied.

Jack and Claire broke out into laughter as they heard Mica yell back, "Beth, please tell me you didn't get these tomatoes from the grocery store. If you did, I ain't eating them."

Shaking her head, she said, "No, honey. I got them yesterday morning when I went to the farmer's market. I believe it's the same guy we got them from last year." Beth took her plate to the table. She opened a bottle of water and took a drink. "Boys, you better eat something before we leave."

The boys rushed into the kitchen. Luckily, Claire and Jack's kitchen was large enough to accommodate them all. Claire loved seeing her family all together, which created moments ranging from laughter to bickering. Regardless, the Klines were a family filled with love for each other, and they had taken Jack in as one of their own. She smiled as she looked upon them, and she felt a moment of happiness.

Today's going to be a good day, she thought.

CHAPTER FOURTEEN

CLAIRE TRIPPED OVER HER PUMPS AS she searched for her cell phone. "Ouch. Crap. Where did I put it?" She threw her silk blouse to the side to hurry before the ringing stopped. She eyed it under her skirt and leaped onto the bed. "Hello?" she said in an out-of-breath tone.

"Claire, honey? Did I wake you?" Beth asked.

"Oh, no mom. I was getting ready for work. I couldn't' find my phone for the life of me."

"Well, I just wanted to tell you how much we enjoyed the Memorial holiday with y'all. We had so much fun on the boat."

"Mom, Jack and I loved having y'all. I miss you already."

Beth laughed. "Your daddy had us up and out of the house by six. We stopped for breakfast at that little café we love so much."

"How far are y'all now, momma?

"We just got on that stupid Natchez Trace again. God love your father, but he drives as slow as Christmas. I was hoping to be home in time to cook dinner, but at this rate, it's going to be pizza for the three of us."

"Beth, I'm sitting right beside you, so I can hear everything you're saying about me." Claire heard her father through the phone.

"Well, I ain't trying to hide it from you. Anyway, I was wondering if you and Jack had plans for the fourth of July?"

"I'm not sure yet. I'll have to talk with Jack first. What're you thinking?"

"Maybe we could all go on a cruise?" Beth asked.

"A cruise? On this short notice?" Claire used one hand to button her blouse. "Mom, I don't think that's possible."

"Well, how about we rent a cabin in the Smokey mountains then?" Beth asked.

"I'm not sure. We'll talk about it, but I'm late for work, so I have to run. Kisses to you, dad, and the boys."

"Of course, dear. Sorry to keep you. We love you, honey." Beth hung up the phone.

Claire dropped the phone back to the bed and finished getting dressed. Then she rushed into the kitchen to grab a quick cup of coffee. She saw Jack's office door open and peeked inside. "Hey, you."

"Hey, BayBay. Come over here and put one right here." He pointed to his lips.

Claire rounded his desk and sat on his lap. She placed her lips gently on his. "Are you sure we have to go to work today?" she asked teasingly. She felt relief as the events from the weekend were behind them, and normalcy seemed to be on the horizon.

"Unfortunately, so. I have to be in court by nine, and then I have two meetings with potential new clients. Maybe we could meet for a late lunch?"

"Can't, I'm doing lunch in one of my offices. I can grab something for dinner on the way home."

"Dinner happens to be my favorite meal." He winked. How does Italian sound? Maybe lasagna?"

"Sounds perfect. I'll pick up a bottle of wine. Red or white?"

"Both." She laughed. As she rose, he slightly pinched her bottom, and she turned her head to his, leaned down, and gave him a kiss. "Jack, I Love you to the moon and back."

"And I love you to the moon and back," he said. "Now, get out of here so we can reconvene for dinner."

"Yes sir, Mr. Lawyer." She laughed as she headed toward the door.

Claire pulled out of the garage at seven-thirty and headed toward the interstate entrance. At a red light, she tapped her fingers impatiently. Then, out of habit, she reached for the knob on the DVD player to load her morning devotional. When she realized what she was doing, she stopped. "Aww, screw it. Might as well listen to it," she said aloud to no one in particular.

As Christians, we believe that no hurt or pain will cross our lives. Jesus himself suffered pain as he was nailed to the cross. The Bible does not guarantee us a life of comfort where all our wants are fulfilled. Why do we think we should no longer face obstacles, just because we're Christians? Our faith is tested throughout our Christian life, and our joys are manifested through our love for Christ. The way you respond to your trials will be a testament of your trust and love in God's plan for you. Don't be defeated, as the devil is a mighty schemer, and he thrives in making you waiver from your faith. Today's bible scripture comes from Psalms 34:17-18. 'The righteous cry out, and the Lord hears them; he delivers them from all their troubles. [18] The Lord is close to the brokenhearted and saves those who are crushed in spirit.'

"Tricky, tricky, tricky," Claire said out loud. "I hear ya, Lord. I hear you."

THE MORNING RUSH hour had delayed her travel by over an hour, and when she pulled into the front parking spot, it was slightly after nine AM. She checked her makeup and reapplied her trusty lip gloss.

She entered her first office with a renewed spirit. "Baby steps, Claire. Baby steps," she whispered to herself. "Good morning Stacy, is there a rep back there already?"

"Hey there, Claire. Good to see ya. Feels like we haven't seen you in a while. How are you and your family? Did y'all have a good holiday?"

"Yes, we did. Thank you for asking. And you?"

"It was peachy. Thanks. Give me a sec and let me check to see if someone is in back. We had a breakfast, but she may have already left."

"Thank you, Stacy." Claire took a seat in the lobby and surveyed the patients in the waiting area. She glanced at her phone and saw that she had a text. *It's from Macy.*

Claire took a deep breath as she read the text from Macy.

M: Hey! Are we okay?

Claire closed her phone. A wave of guilt hit her like a block of bricks. Claire closed her eyes and silently counted to five.

Claire heard someone clear her throat, and she looked up and saw Stacy motioning for her to come to the counter. Claire put her phone away and walked to the counter. "You can go on back to the sample closet. The doc should be around shortly. Good seeing you, Claire." The receptionist picked up the ringing phone.

Claire nodded and made her way past the nurses' station. The sample closet was situated in the back of the hall directly across from several patient rooms. She pulled the samples from her bag and stacked them neatly in their designated spot. She pulled out her iPad to pre-plan her detail and load the sample count in for his signature.

She heard his voice boom, "Be right with you" and glanced up to see the doctor wave to her as he entered a patient's room.

She had hoped to catch him before he entered, but this allowed her some time to catch up on work emails. She checked her email and groaned. One hundred and fifty emails filled her inbox. She rapidly went through the subject lines and deleted the non-essentials. She paid specific attention to an email from her manager:

Hey Team, it's that time of year! Our 1st half POA meeting is coming up at the end of July. I am excited to announce that we will be going to Tampa! Now, that being said, I need you all to schedule your flights by EOD Friday, with Lucas Travel Company. Please see their contact information below along with your travel details. As you can see, the rooms have been booked on the corporate account. And better yet, no roommates will be happening this year. The only expense you will need to put on your Amex is your flights and food during travel days. Over the next few days, I will be sending your pre-work as well."

Claire closed the email. "Crap," she said quietly.

She had completely forgotten about the upcoming POA. She took a deep breath and exhaled. Claire felt the ugly dread radiate up through her stomach. "Nope, not happening." She swallowed and refocused.

She hadn't seen many of the sales representatives on her team since January, and she was pregnant then. She pictured the whole scenario in her head—everyone debating on what they should say and tip toeing around her like she may break. Claire's brain worked overtime wondering if she could figure out a way to skip the POA when the doctor entered the sample closet.

CLAIRE PULLED INTO the garage that evening with Alfonzo's famous family dinner package. She had gotten lasagna, breadsticks, salad, and tiramisu. When she walked through the front door, she heard soft music resonating through the kitchen. A smile emerged on her face, and she kicked her heels off to the side while shifting the bag of food. She walked into the kitchen, and her eyes were instantly drawn to the dining room table. She drew in a quick breath. In the middle of the table, two candles flickered beside a vase of roses. She saw two bottles of wine chilling on the table.

God, I love this man," she thought as her heart skipped a slight beat. She wanted so desperately to give him children. Her mind reeled around the moment, and she took a deep breath. *No. I'll enjoy this night with my husband. I will not cry, I will not be sad, I will be attentive to his needs, and I will relish in his love for me.*

"Jack, I'm home." Claire turned to the counter and sat her purse and the food down. "Jack?" She made her way to their bedroom and opened the door. Immediately, she saw rose petals spread on the carpet with a trail leading to their bed. "Jack?"

"Hey BayBay, I'm in here."

Claire went into the bathroom, and there he was. He stood by the tub, which he had filled with bubbles and rose petals. He motioned for her to come closer, and she followed his lead. "Jack?" she asked questioningly.

"Get undressed and climb into the tub. I'll bring you a glass of wine." He leaned down to kiss her lips. She felt a flutter in her stomach.

"All this Jack?"

"All of this is for you, BayBay." He winked at her.

She could only nod. She undressed and slid into the tub. She could smell the rose petals as the bubbles soothed her skin. She heard the music, and she stretched her legs out. Jack entered the bathroom with a glass of wine.

"Here, my lady," he said as he mockingly bowed.

"Why thank you, sir." Claire took the glass. She looked at him, and she saw his forgiveness. "Jack, thank you for forgiving me for my behavior over the weekend."

"Always, Claire. You're the light of my life," he responded softly.

"You're amazing; you know that, right?"

He sat down on the edge of the tub and put the tip of his finger into the bathtub. "So I have been told by many." He laughed lightly.

"Many, huh?" she asked in a teasing voice.

"Yes, many." He laughed louder and leaned over the bathtub to kiss her. "BayBay, you're my one and only; you know that. When God placed you in my life, it was toast for all the others. You won my heart forever."

"Jack, can I ask you something without it ruining the moment?"

"Anything."

"Will you love me even if I can't have children? I want to give you a child so much."

"Claire, I will love you until the moment of my last breath. If you and I cannot have a biological child, then we'll adopt. Either way Claire, it's you and me, babe."

She nodded as tears filled her eyes. Jack was a kind man, and she knew he deserved more than she could give him. Claire took a deep breath. "Jack?"

"Yes."

"Will you still love me if I can't find faith again?"

"Claire, your faith is not lost forever. You're angry, and you're letting that anger interrupt your love for Jesus, but you'll get it back. I'm sorry I haven't been more patient."

She nodded again. Jack stroked her hair and handed her a bath cloth. "I love you, Jack."

"And I you. Now that we have established that we love each other," he said jokingly, "I'll go put that ravishingly delicious dinner you slaved over on the table."

"Ha, you and your jokes." She took a sip of her wine

and closed her eyes. Claire relished in the moment and let the day slip by.

After the water cooled, she went into the kitchen and saw him seated at the table. He rose from the table and went to her chair. He pulled her chair out, she sat down, and he scooted her forward.

"My lady, what may I serve you first?" He motioned to the Lasagna and salad on the table.

"Why sir, I will have both, please." She sparked a smile at his antics.

"Of course, my lady. Salad and lasagna coming up. Would you like more wine as well?"

"Yes, please."

He poured them both a glass of wine and sat in his chair. He reached for her hand and took it. Claire stiffened slightly as he prayed. "Dear Lord, we give grace for this food we are about to partake upon. We ask You will bless our bodies and thank You for allowing us to be together tonight as a family. Amen."

"Amen," she said as well, and Claire noticed Jack's eyebrow rise in response. Claire took a bite of her salad. "How was your day?"

He looked up from a huge bite of lasagna. "It was great. We picked the jury, and the trial starts in a few weeks. I think I'll be able to win this one fairly easy."

"That's amazing, Jack. Can you tell me about the case?"

"Well, you know I can't give you any specific details, but the gist is that my client was charged with kidnapping by taking her child from the father." His attention went back to his food.

"Oh, no. Did she tell you why she did it? Was the father abusive?"

"Maybe. Or, that's what she believed. Anyway, that's enough about my day. How was yours?" he asked lovingly.

"It was good, I suppose. The only interesting thing was I got an email about our POA meeting. We're going to Tampa this time."

"Cool. When are y'all going?"

"The last week of July. We're supposed to return home on August 2nd."

"Did they give you the option to extend or travel early?" he asked as he took another huge bite of lasagna.

She nodded and chewed her food.

"So, do you think we could squeeze in a few days as a trip for us if my trial has ended by then? Maybe we could invite Macy and David?"

She cringed at hearing him bring up Macy. "Ugh. I haven't spoken to Macy since the cookout."

"Well, I know she's left four messages on our machine," Jack said.

"I know. She called my cell a bunch and sent me a few texts. I just haven't called her back yet." She took a sip of her wine.

"Claire, she's your best friend. You're going to have to talk to her eventually."

"I know," Claire replied. "I'm just torn between feeling bad for the way I talked to her that day and still not wanting to hear her preach to me about the things that I 'need' to do."

"Well, she has your best interest in heart. I really think you should talk to her," Jack said.

"I will." Diverting the conversation, she changed the subject. "Anyway, yes, I think we could possibly use my POA meeting as a trip. It's been a while since we've taken a trip, and it'd be fun. How large is your caseload for June and July?" she asked.

"It's fairly large, but I could shift some things around. One of the Juniors could handle some things. Actually, we just got a new Junior partner." Jack had made partner last year, and his workload had decreased slightly. As a junior partner, he worked sixty-five hours a week—and often missed dinner with Claire. Now at thirty-two, he was the youngest partner in the firm, with the other partners being founder partners.

"Really? What's his name?" Claire asked through a bite of salad.

"Chad Taylor." Jack spooned more lasagna onto his plate. "Very smart guy. He just graduated number one in his class from the top law school in Texas."

"Mmmm." She swallowed. "Sounds impressive."

Jack shook his head. "Our recruiter went after him hard to get him to Nashville," Jack said.

"Wow, he must be good."

"He has a very promising future." Jack loaded his fork with salad. "Really nice guy too."

"Single?" Claire asked with mischief in her eye.

"Claire!" Jack used a heavy southern drawl.

She winked at her husband. "Well, you know Gabby needs a good man."

"Really! You think Gabby would want you meddling in her love life?"

Claire shrugged. "It's sisterly love."

"Mmmm hmm. You keep thinking that," he said with a smirk.

Claire laughed at her husband. Dinner felt normal, and she was thankful for a bit of normalcy. "So back to my POA. Do you think we could make it a short getaway as well?"

"Some fun in the sun, with you? I'm game!" he said excitedly.

She smiled at Jack. "Okay. Let's do it."

"Awesome, "Jack said. "We could extend our stay past the second of August, possibly. So, what about asking David and Macy to go?"

"I think we should. I promise I'm going to clear the air with Macy this week."

"Okay. I'm meeting David for lunch tomorrow. Can I go ahead and mention it to him?"

"Yep. That'll give me extra incentive to talk to Macy."

After dinner, Jack cleared the table as Claire filled the dishwasher with dirty dishes.

Suddenly, she felt Jack standing behind her, and his arms wrapped around her waist. "Hey. Wanna meet me in the movie room for a movie and some popcorn?"

Hairs on her arms shivered, as his breath was hot. "Only if you bring up the tiramisu." She turned to meet his eyes.

"You're on. Tiramisu, a movie with me and my girl. What could be better?"

She leaned in to kiss him. "How about this?"

"Hmmm. That might be better. Try that again." He wrapped his arms around her and kissed her deeply. He pulled his lips away from hers. "I'll even let you pick the movie," he said cooingly.

"Okay. I'll meet you upstairs, and don't forget extra butter on my popcorn."

CHAPTER FIFTEEN

CLAIRE SAT IN HER CAR LOOKING AT HER phone. The screen was blank, and she was hesitant to touch it. "Get it together, Claire. Get it together," she told herself. She exhaled out loud and touched the message button. She scrolled down the list and found Macy's name. She hovered over Macy's name and hesitated before clicking it. She inhaled and began the text.

C: Hey! Remember me?

Claire waited anxiously as she watched the little bubbles.

M: Hey you! How are you?
C: I'm good. How are you?
M: Busy as always. It's been a little too long, right?

That was Macy, as straight to the point as possible. Claire felt embarrassed that she had let the silence linger between them.

C: Yep!

M: I'm glad you text me.
C: Me too. I'm sorry, Macy.
M: Me too!
C: You don't need to be. Could we meet for coffee/lunch today or tomorrow?"

Claire waited, hoping that Macy would respond. After a few, long minutes, Macy texted her back.

M: Sorry, had to tend to the kids. I'm back. YEAAASSSS PLEASSSEEE . . . I NEED COFFEEEEEEE!!! AND FOOOOOD!!!! STARVING HERE!!!!!
C: LOL. Today or Tomorrow?
M: Let's do it today! I can meet you at noon-ish! Where?
C: HAL'S Cafe?
M: Works!!! See you soon! And you're buying!"

Claire sent Macy a thumbs-up symbol, and then she sent Jack a quick text.

C: Hey!!! Meeting Macy for coffee/lunch today!!! I think we'll be okay!! Love you bunches!
J: Awesome! Love you! I'm headed back to court! Dinner?
C: How about we meet at Lilly's? 6:30?
J: Sounds like a plan. I'll meet you there. Gotta go. Love you!
C: Love you!

She put her phone away. Claire looked at her watch and realized she had enough time to make a few more office calls before she met Macy for lunch and a cup of coffee.

CLAIRE PULLED INTO the parking spot closest to the door of HAL'S Cafe, a local favorite. It was situated on a corner lot with a white wrap-around porch. She smiled as she saw the porch patrons chatting. They seemed peaceful and relaxed in their conversation. She and Jack came to HAL'S almost every Saturday morning before starting their day.

She surveyed the parking lot and saw Macy's grey minivan parked in the corner. She exited the car and walked into the main room. She looked around and saw Macy waving her arms in the air frantically. She waved back and smiled at her friend. Macy looked beautiful; she had her hair in a messy bun, and she wore a pink sundress. As she walked up to the small table, Macy stood and hugged her tightly.

"There you are!" Macy squeezed so hard that Claire barely could breathe.

"Too tight," Claire responded and laughed.

"Oops." Macy laughed as she released her friend.

"You look beautiful," Claire said.

Macy blushed and did a small twirl. "It's new. I ordered it online. And it fits! Boom!" Macy laughed zealously.

Claire laughed. "Well, it's absolutely adorable on you. Which place did you order it from?"

"Some site called Jesse's," she said shrugging.

Claire nodded and sat down. "I think I've ordered from them before. Regardless, pink is definitely your color."

"Awe! You're a darling." She reached for Claire's hand. "Oh, how I have missed you, my friend."

"I've missed you too." Claire looked down embarrassed.

"Don't do that."

"Don't do what?" she asked Macy.

"Don't act like we can't make a mistake. Did you think you could run me off? I'm your best friend, and you're mine. We had a fight. Big deal!" she said nonchalantly.

"How do you do that?" Claire asked curiously. "How do you forgive so easily without any questions or without apologies?"

"It's called grace, my sweet friend. Grace is given to us, and as Christians, we are to give grace to others. Grace is not optional, and grace does not mean we should be treated poorly, but grace opens the door for forgiveness."

Claire suppressed her urge to roll her eyes.

They both looked up as the waitress came to the table. "Hi, I'm Maria. What can I get you both?"

"I'll have a decaf with half and half," Claire answered.

"And you?" The waitress turned her attention to Macy.

"I'll have a green tea, please," Macy said.

Claire arched her eyebrow at her friend. "Seriously? Green tea? Who are you?"

Macy laughed loudly. "I'll have you know I'm trying to be more plant-based in my diet."

"Plant-based?" Claire tilted her head awkwardly. She was relieved that they seem to be on a normal track to their friendship again. She had missed Macy.

"Yes, plant-based. It's all about eating healthy and eating plant-based items." Macy wrinkled her nose slightly and winked playfully with her right eye.

"Macy, you live in the South. It's all about eating fried chicken, mashed potatoes, beans, and cornbread."

They both laughed as Claire overly stated her southern accent. The waitress sat their drinks on the table.

"Are you ready to order?" the waitress asked.

Claire looked at her menu. "I'll have the tuna salad sandwich, please."

"Do you want fruit or chips?"

"Chips. Thanks," Claire said as she handed the menu to the waitress.

"And you?" The waitress turned her attention to Macy.

Macy took a deep breath and concentrated on the menu. "Hmmm, choices."

Claire laughed gently at her friend. Since the day Claire had met Macy, she took forever when making food choices.

"What specials do you have today?" Macy asked.

"We have hummus with pita chips, fried chicken tender salad with a homemade dressing, and peach cobbler." The waitress tapped her pencil to her pad.

"Yeah, none of those for sure." Macy laughed. She looked down at her menu again.

"Any day now . . ." Claire spoke.

Macy looked at her friend and laughed. "Always in a hurry, are we?"

"Would you like me to come back?" the waitress asked.

Macy let out a gently soft laugh. "Of course not, dear. I'll have a club sandwich with no tomatoes, on rye bread."

The waitress made the notes and left the table.

"After all that time, you only picked a club sandwich, which is only partially plant-based?" Claire teased.

"Well, food choices should not be made lightly, my dear." Macy winked again.

Claire paused for a moment and studied her hands. "I'm sorry for how I treated you on Memorial Day. It was cruel, and I should have never been so ugly toward you."

Macy looked at Claire before she spoke. Claire sensed something was coming. "I forgive you, Claire, but that doesn't mean you can treat me that way again."

Claire nodded. "I know. I've become a stranger to myself, Jack, my family, and now my friends."

"Claire, have you prayed lately?"

Claire, shocked by her question, hesitated, and took a sip of her coffee. *Breathe,* she thought. *Don't yell at her. Don't be angry.* "No, I haven't—not since the hospital."

"Not at all?" Macy looked shocked.

"Well, not individually per se. Jack has prayed for us, my parents have prayed for us, but not me." She shrugged her shoulders.

"Why?" Macy asked intently.

"Why? Seriously, Macy?"

"Yes, Seriously."

Claire thought of the many reasons she had stopped praying. "Because God turned His back on me. Because God let my child die in my womb. Because I am . . ." She trailed off.

"Because you are what?"

"Because I am lost," Claire answered quietly.

Macy took Claire's hand, and Claire didn't resist. "John 13:7 says: 'What I am doing you do not understand now, but afterward you will understand.'" Macy searched Claire's eyes for understanding. "Do you see? Do you see that He is working in your life, Claire? Do you feel His presence?"

Claire blew out a breath. "Macy, can I tell you something?"

"Of course, you can."

Claire inhaled deeply. "I think I heard a male voice speaking to me." She waited for a reaction. Macy made none. "The voice speaking to me . . . it's almost like it's God," Claire said hesitantly. "Does that sound crazy?"

"No. Not at all," Macy replied. "When did you hear the voice?" she asked with no surprise in her voice.

"First time was in the hospital, and then the second time was in my bedroom."

"What did the voice say to you?" Macy leaned on her elbows closer to Claire.

Claire situated in her chair and took a sip of her coffee. She cleared her throat, "It said, 'Claire, I am here. I love you, my child.'" She looked at Macy.

"Did this voice say anything else?" Macy asked curiously.

Claire nodded, "Yeah. It said, 'I have never left you, and your child is my child.'"

"You remembered exactly what the voice said while you were under that much stress?"

Again, Claire nodded. "Well yeah. It's not every day that I hear a random voice when no one is there. I don't know. Maybe I'm going crazy."

"No. You're not going crazy. This is amazing, Claire. You were under so much stress with the miscarriage. How much do you remember about that day?" Macy asked.

"What?" Claire asked confused.

"What else is vivid in your memory?"

"From that day? Not much, beyond losing my baby. Everything seems a blur. The hurt is the only memory I have. It never leaves me."

Macy leaned in further. "Don't you see, Claire? Do you see the blessing you have been given?"

"Blessing?"

"He was speaking to you Claire, and you *listened*. You verbatim just repeated what He said. It *was* verbatim, right?"

Claire nodded.

"Honey." Macy took her hand and squeezed gently. "God is with you, and He is trying to speak to you. What an amazing, amazing miracle you are experiencing."

"Miracle? My baby died. If it *is* God, then I don't know why He's trying to talk to me. I'm mad at Him. And honestly, I've been purposely avoiding talking to Him. Besides, I don't really think it's God. I just don't know what it all means," Claire said.

"It means you need to get down on your knees and pray. You need to find out what He is trying to say to you. You need to grow in your relationship and stop this foolishness of being anti-Jesus. We all know you're a Christian, and I know you better than this. You're a fighter, and as a fighter, you need to step up your game and fight for your relationship with your Savior."

Claire sat quietly as she digested Macy's words.

CHAPTER SIXTEEN

As Claire entered the Nephrology clinic, she studied the patient waiting room. It was crowded today, and she felt empathy for those waiting. She pulled her sample bag behind her and made her way to the receptionist's desk.

The receptionist wore her hair high in a bun and had glasses on the bridge of her nose. "Good morning," the receptionist said. "May I help you?"

"Hi, I am Claire St. John. Are there any reps back?"

"Have you registered with the vendor book?" the receptionist asked.

Claire nodded gently. "Yes, I've been here on several occasions. I don't believe we've met."

The receptionist smiled. "No, this is my first week here. I'm Jenna Thomas." She held up a finger for Claire to pause as she answered the phone. "Mallory Nephrology—let me transfer you. Turning her attention back to Claire, she said, "Sorry about that. The phone is ringing off the hook today."

"No worries. Is it okay if I go on back?" Claire asked.

"Sure. Doctor Miller isn't here today."

"Thanks. Which docs are in?" Claire asked.

"Hamilton, Jones, and Weigel," she said looking at her computer.

"Thank you." Claire placed a jar of candy on her counter alongside her business card. "Enjoy."

"Awesome, thank you. Nice to meet you, Claire."

"You too, Jenna," Claire said as she entered the door.

AN HOUR AND A half later, Claire exited the Nephrology Clinic. She opened the doors, and the sunshine hit her face. She reached into her large tote and dug around to find her sunglasses. As she was digging around, someone bumped into her. Claire looked up and recognized the familiar face.

"Oh, I'm so sorry. I was in such a hurry, I didn't see you," the woman said.

"Nurse Reese?" Claire asked.

"Hi. Claire, right?"

"Yep, it's me. I knew I recognized you."

"It's good to see you again." Reese's eyes were swollen and red.

"You as well. Are you okay?" Claire asked.

"I should be asking you that. It's been what, three months since your miscarriage?" Reese blew her nose with a tissue.

"Yes." Claire nodded. "But we don't have to talk about that. You're obviously upset. You want to talk about it?" Claire motioned toward the bench in front of the clinic.

Reese looked apprehensive. "Are you sure?"

"Of course." They sat down on the bench, and a moment passed. "So, what's going on?" Were you coming from the clinic?"

Reese swallowed back tears. "Yes. I was here for a follow-up visit." She blew her nose again.

"Is there any way I can help?"

"Not unless you have a kidney to give." Reese laughed awkwardly.

"A kidney? You need a new kidney?" Claire asked surprised. Reese nodded. "Two."

"When did you find out?" Claire asked.

"Three weeks ago. I went in due to some issues, and bam. Just like that, I need two new kidneys." Reese pressed her lips together. "I still have both of my kidneys, but they're slowly failing."

Claire watched as Reese tried to compose herself. "Wow, I'm so sorry. What are your next steps?"

Reese blew her nose again. "They put me on a donor list, but that takes forever, and the doctor said that my time is limited. So, I guess I need to find a donor kidney before both of my kidneys fail."

"What about your family? Have you had them tested for a match?"

Reese nodded. "Yes, but I was adopted. So, it's not likely they'll be a match, and I never met my birth parents."

"Oh, wow," Claire said shocked.

"Yeah. So, it looks like I'm waiting for a miracle from the National Donor Transplant list." Reese shrugged. "I'm only twenty-nine years old. I don't drink, I don't do drugs, and I'm a nurse. I just don't understand how this happens to someone so healthy. The whole thing just came out of nowhere, and I'm just reeling." Reese paused and inhaled a deep breath. She exhaled loudly. "I'm not scared to die. I just have so much I want to do before I go."

"Life doesn't make much sense sometimes." Claire paused not sure what to do. She felt her heart stir with conviction. *How do I help her?* Claire thought. "Reese, I don't mean to be bold, but do you know the Lord?"

Reese studied Claire. "Yes. I'm a Christian."

Claire nodded.

"Are you?" Reese asked.

"Since I was a child. But . . ."

"But?"

"Well, since I had the miscarriage, I haven't communicated with Him much." Claire pointed to the sky.

"I get it. Hurt sometimes overpowers our ability to let the pain go. I've witnessed that with many of my patients."

Claire stared out onto the parking lot. "Do you think you'll lose your faith?"

Reese paused and waited a few moments before answering. "I've just been hit with the knowledge that I may or may not survive this kidney disease. But all I know to do is to pull closer to God for comfort. He's my father, and He loves me." She studied Claire's profile and saw the tension on her face. "Okay. It's my time to be bold. Can I ask *you* a question?"

Claire turned her attention back to Reese. "Okay."

"Do you want to continue your relationship with Jesus? Or are you ready to relinquish your faith?"

Shocked by the question, Claire felt guilt and embarrassment creep up her spine. "What did you say?"

Reese, unfazed by her tone, pushed harder. "What are *you* going to do? Are you going to keep pushing through life with Jesus in it, or you going to give it up and become a deist?"

"A Deist?" What in the world is a deist?" Claire asked confused.

Reese let out a gentle laugh. "A deist is someone who believes there is a God but doesn't follow a religious path. Is that who you've become since your miscarriage?"

"Wow, that *was* bold," Claire responded.

"That tends to be my nature. Plus, I have nothing to lose, it seems," Reese said.

"Of course not. I don't . . ." Claire blew out air. "I'm angry at Him. I'm mad." Claire rubbed her hands through her blonde hair. "It's not fair to say that I've lost my faith completely because I have faith that He could have saved my baby. I believe that God is all-powerful, and He could have intervened. I just . . . I don't know. I feel abandoned by Him." She paused. "I don't know how to explain it well. I have all these emotions bundled up, and I always feel like I'm going to explode."

Reese nodded in acknowledgment.

"Are you not mad about your diagnosis?" Claire asked.

"Of course, I'm mad, but that doesn't change my love for God. It makes me want to lean in further. He's my rock and my salvation. And with Him, all things are possible. It's having faith.

Faith . . ." Claire thought for a moment. "I still have faith. I know God loves me." She looked up to the sky and closed her eyes. "I just don't understand why."

"Actually, that's normal. In my career as a nurse, I've seen so much pain, so much death. And I've actually been asked that question many times. Why? Why does God let bad things happen to good people? And I don't have the answer. I don't think anyone does. But I do know that God loves us, and He wants to comfort us. And if we have faith in Him, the next life . . . well, it's nothing to be afraid of." She paused for a moment, and then she laughed. "Wow. I guess I need to listen to the advice that I've been giving to other people."

"We're a mess, aren't we?" Claire laughed gently. "It's our second time to meet, and both times have been filled with a tragedy."

Reese laughed. "I suppose we are a mess. But thank you for talking to me. I feel so much better. I just needed a reminder that it's all going to be okay—no matter what happens. And you just helped me realize that." She paused again. "Wow. I think God brought us into each other's lives for a purpose."

"I suppose He did." Claire looked at Reese.

Reese looked at her watch. "Okay. I have to run, or I'll be late for my shift at the ER. But thanks again for listening. And seriously, think about your faith. Life is too short to let the anger control us."

Claire stood up and hugged her. "I'm sorry about your kidneys. The man upstairs might not be listening to me right now, but I'm going to pray for you."

Reese stood back. "Really?"

"Yeah," Claire said. "I think I will."

"Thank you," Reese said. "Maybe we'll see each other again."

"I hope so Reese," Claire said.

Claire watched as Reese walked off. *How did I get to*

this place, Lord? How? How do I find my way back to you? Claire thought.

The sky was clear and still, but Claire felt her long blonde hair gently blow, and the hair on her arms stood as shiver riveted throughout her body. "God?" Suddenly, sobs escaped her lips. She lifted her hands to the sky and called out "Are you here with me?"

"Claire, I am here. I love you, my child," the male voice answered.

No longer startled by the voice, Claire closed her eyes. *"Dear Lord, forgive me. Please take care of Reese and provide her comfort. I've been so angry about my loss, and here she is on the brink of facing her own death, even after she has comforted the sick and dying. My anger seems so insignificant. I'm so sorry for everything I've done since losing my baby. I still don't know why, and I'm still so sad, God. But I trust You. I trust that You'll heal me. I'm sorry for not trusting You faithfully. I'm sorry for hurting Jack, my family, and my friends. I'm sorry for not leaning on You. I haven't ever needed you more than I do now. Please, please forgive me. And I know you sent Reese to give me perspective. Thank you for putting her in my life.*

Claire felt a breeze rush across her face, and she heard the familiar male voice. *"Claire, I love you, my child. You are forgiven."*

CHAPTER SEVENTEEN

"OH, LOOK AT THOSE GORGEOUS PALM TREES," Macy said excitedly as the Uber driver took them down the highway.

"Claire and I love Tampa. The culture and the beaches are amazing. You two are going to have so much fun." Jack turned from the front seat to see his friends.

"I, for one, am excited to see the beaches. It's been over a year since we've been close to the ocean. We took the kids to Panama City last year for a family vacation." David placed his sunglasses high on his head and rummaged in Macy's purse.

"Well, I'm excited to spend time with Claire," Macy said.

"I was a little worried about y'all for a while there," Jack said.

"Naw, Jack. You oughtta know that nothing can break up me and Claire. It's girl power. The force is strong."

David and Jack laughed at Macy's tone. When the Uber driver came to a stop, they saw Claire in blue Bermuda shorts and a white top, standing under the porte-cochère. Her blonde ponytail bounced up and down with her flailing arms.

"You're here! You're here! Finally!" Claire ran to Jack and jumped as he caught her in his arms. "Oh, I am so happy to see you."

"Hey BayBay, did you miss me?"

"Not at all." She laughed, and he kissed her longingly.

"Ahem . . ." Macy cleared her throat. "And hello to us?"

Claire giggled and jumped down from Jack's arms. "Hello, my Macy. Come here." She extended her arms, and they hugged. As she released Macy from their hug, she joined hands with Jack. "Hey, David."

"Hi Claire, good to see you. You look like you got some sun."

"Yep. I had some pool time today and plenty of beach time after sessions. The weather has been amazing this week, and it's supposed to continue through our stay."

"Oh, I am so excited. Sunshine here I come," Macy yelled.

Claire laughed. "Come on I'll show y'all in."

The hotel was a rendition of a nineteen-twenties-era hotel. Old replicas and a diamond-shaped flooring whelmed the lobby. The stately white columns engulfed the area as windows overlooked the ocean, allowing a breeze to sweep through the lobby. A jazz musician played his saxophone, filling the space with lively music.

"Wow, this is gorgeous." Macy opened her mouth in awe.

"It *is* amazing. They have golf carts that look like mini Rolls-Royces, bikes we can reserve to ride along the paths, and a rooftop bar area that overlooks the ocean. And the restaurant has some of the best food this side of Tampa," Claire rambled as she led them to the check-in counter. "We are in room 2222. I really hope y'all are close."

"Me too," Macy chimed.

Macy and Claire giggled as the hostess handed them a glass of sparkling water. "Cheers," they said in unison.

Jack laughed lightly at the two women. They seemed so young and free with their silly giggles. He was excited to see Claire smiling. *Maybe my Claire is finally back,* he thought. "Let's all meet back down at six. We can grab dinner and maybe go for a walk on the beach. Sound good?"

"Sounds like a plan." David looked at his room key. "We are in room 2267. Not too far from y'all." David slid the key into his pocket.

"Perfect," Claire said, and she high-fived Macy as they walked to the elevator.

"They're on cloud nine, aren't they? Claire looks so happy." David laughed.

"They sure are. It's been over three months since we lost the baby, and she seems to finally be on the right track." Jack smiled.

"That's great," David said.

IN THE HOTEL room, Jack said, "So, this has been your home for the last few days." He looked around at the room and approved. Decorated in pale yellows and blues, the room had windows that directly faced the ocean. He crossed to the window and stared at the water. The waves crashed onto the sand and then rolled back to the ocean. "I love the ocean. It's so powerful."

"Beautiful, isn't it?"

"Yes, BayBay, it is. Come over here to me." He

extended his arm, and she took it. They held hands as they watched the beach activity.

"I'm so glad you're here, Jack. I missed you." She squeezed his hand.

"You know I missed you too." Suddenly, he looked seriously into her eyes. "I don't know what I'd do without you. It's absolutely insane how much I love you."

She could see the love pouring from his eyes, and her heart melted at the sight. "Jack, I'll never leave you. I promise." She closed her eyes as he leaned in to kiss her.

Claire was super excited to surprise Jack with the news that she had won Pinnacle, which is the highest sales award given by her company. She had also been awarded Sales Representative of the year, which meant she would be getting a nice monetary payout for the year. As the recipient of the Pinnacle Award, she and Jack would attend the company-paid trip to Paris. She planned to tell him after dinner. Paris was a dream vacation that she and Jack had wanted to take since college.

"So do tell. Who won Pinnacle this year?" Jack led Claire to the sofa.

Claire bit her lower lip, debating whether to tell him. "Will you be disappointed if it isn't me?"

"BayBay, seriously?" he asked raising his eyebrow. "I would never be disappointed in you."

She laughed gently, as she could see the excitement drooling from his lips. "Alright, Alright. Give me a drum roll please."

"DDDDDDDDDDDD"

"And the 2018 Pinnacle Winner is . . ." She hesitated to encourage the suspense.

"Any day now."

"I won, Jack!"

"No way! Seriously?"

"Seriously." He kissed her, pressing her lips deeply. She murmured during the kiss. "Air, Jack. I need Air."

He laughed. "Oops. The excitement got me."

"I can tell." Her laughed filled the room.

"So where is the trip? Did they announce it?" he asked.

"Jack Hudson St. John . . ."

"Oooh, this must be serious. You used my full name." He batted his eyes.

"Do you want to know or not?"

"Of course, I do."

"Then be quiet and let me finish." She laughed as he hung his head in a pout. "I am excited to tell you that we will be taking an all-expense-paid trip to . . . Paris." She smiled in anticipation of his response.

"Paris, Tennessee?" He laughed, and she snorted loudly at him.

"Real funny. Come on, Jack. How excited are you right now?"

"It's amazing. I am *so* proud of you. We finally get to take the trip of our dreams! Woohoo!"

"I know! I can't believe it. Paris. I was going to surprise you tonight after dinner."

He shrugged. "Who needs to wait that long for some good news! So, when is the trip?"

"It's next April, which gives us plenty of time to plan what we want to do."

"Yep, and that gives me time to shift some cases around," he said.

Her phone rang and interrupted her thoughts. She looked for her purse to find her phone.

"I guarantee you it's your mom." Jack stretched his feet out on the sofa.

Claire grabbed her phone and nodded to Jack. "You are correct. Mom, Hi."

"Well, there you are, Claire. Goodness, I've been calling you for two days now. You do know your mother's number, don't you?" Beth asked in a snipping voice.

"Yes, mom. I've been busy with work. I'm sorry."

"I guess I'll forgive you this time. Anyway, did Jack make it in?"

"Yep, he's here. They arrived about forty minutes ago."

"Hey momma Beth," Jack called from the couch. Claire rolled her eyes at Jack. He had always been a suck-up to her mom.

"Tell him hello, dear."

"Jack, mom says hi." She snarled at his grin.

"Well, I called to tell you that your father and I are getting a divorce."

Claire coughed "What!"

"What is it?" Jack looked concerned.

"I'm joking, Claire. But now that I have your undivided attention, we can discuss the real reason I called."

Claire shook her head at Jack. "Seriously mom, you thought that was the best way to get my attention? What is wrong with you today?"

Beth sighed, realizing that Claire had not found her humor funny. "Would you calm down? I was only joking. Now, what I called about was Thanksgiving."

"Mom, it's July."

"Claire, I'm not stupid. I know what month it is."

"I don't think you're stupid, mom. Are you feeling okay?"

"Why yes, honey, I feel perfectly fine. Stop trying to patronize me and listen." Beth seemed slightly irritated. "Now back to Thanksgiving."

Claire shrugged her shoulders to Jack and mouthed the word *Thanksgiving*.

"This year, your father and I are taking a trip and will not be home for Thanksgiving. I've already told the boys and Gabby because they actually answer the phone when I call."

"Huh? Your skipping Thanksgiving? Again mom, are you alright?"

"Claire, you're never too old to respect your mother. Now mind your manners. I feel perfectly fine, thank you."

"Mom, I'm sorry. It's been a long week. So, let's see, y'all are taking a trip to where?"

"We're going to Colorado. To ski," Beth said matter-of-factly.

"Ski? Seriously, mom, are y'all not too old for that?" Claire's ears hurt from the huff that vibrated the phone. "Sorry mom, I shouldn't have said that. But you and dad thrive on holidays. It's always been such an important part of our family time."

"No Claire, you shouldn't have asked if we are too old. But if you must know, Dad and I have always wanted to go skiing. And by George, it's time."

"Okay, so I guess that's awesome y'all are going. So, what're the boys and Gabby doing for Thanksgiving?

"Well, my eldest daughter, that's where you come in."

Claire shook her head. Jack's eyes danced with laughter as he watched. "Don't even go there. You know I can't cook."

"I know that, which is embarrassing for a southern woman, but we'll save that one for another day. Anyway, Daddy and I have decided that we'll cater Thanksgiving at your home for all our children to spend the holiday together."

"Mom, Jack and I can afford to cater Thanksgiving. You know this right?"

"Of course, I know this, Claire. Again, I'm not stupid. But to not feel guilty about leaving my children on the holiday, we will provide the full-course meal."

Claire shrugged her shoulders and mouthed to Jack, "We are hosting Thanksgiving." Jack gave a thumbs up.

"Claire, are you still there?"

"Yes, Mom sorry. Poor service, I suppose. Jack and I will be excited to host Thanksgiving."

"Heck yeah! Sounds fun." Jack rang out from the couch. He snapped his fingers at Claire to get her attention. "It's five-fifteen. We're meeting David and Macy at six, remember?" Jack whispered.

"Mom, gotta go. We're gonna be late for our dinner reservations."

"Okay Honey, we can talk more about Thanksgiving in a few weeks."

"Sounds good, mom. I love you."

"Claire Bear, Daddy and I love you." Beth hung up the phone.

Claire shook her head and placed the phone on the desk.

"Whew, what was that?" Jack asked.

"Yeah, not sure. Skiing? You think this might be a mid-life crisis?" Claire asked puzzled.

"Possibly. You know parents do strange things as they age."

"True." She smiled, and their eyes locked. She bit her lower lip, "Jack, enough of talking about my parents. Wanna help me get ready?"

"Yeah, I could do that," Jack said getting up and walking toward the bathroom. His heart raced with excitement as he saw her clothing fall to the floor. He moaned silently as he closed the bathroom door.

CHAPTER EIGHTEEN

JACK AND DAVID SCOOTED THE CHAIRS OUT as Macy and Claire took a seat.

"Such gentlemen," Claire responded.

"I know right." Macy winked at her husband.

"Well, our mothers did teach us how to treat a lady," Jack spoke.

"Maybe you should remember that when we are back home," Claire picked.

Jack shot her a look.

"Alright, smarty pants," Macy, interrupted holding her sparkling water high. "I would like to make a toast." She waited as they grabbed their glasses. "I would like to toast our friendship. No one could ever deny that this friendship of ours was a part of God's plan. Jesus knew what he was doing when He brought us four together. I could not fathom having a friendship built around Christ any greater than this one."

"Here-Here," Jack and David said.

Claire's eyes shone with tears glistening in the moonlight. "I love each of you dearly, and I am so thankful for your friendship."

The two women hugged each other as the men shook their heads. "Such emotion," Jack said jokingly.

"Hey, now. Give us a break. Look at this view, and tomorrow, we will be laying out on the sand soaking up the rays." Macy sighed.

The waiter appeared and took their orders. Claire decided to have the swordfish and was sharing potatoes with Jack. Macy and David both had the Tuna, and Jack went for turf and surf. Their meal was delicious, and as they ate, they chatted amiably. Each told stories of past times that lead to laughter and joking throughout the meal.

As the waiter cleared the table, Macy pushed her chair back slightly and placed her hand over her stomach. "I'm stuffed." She blew out a breath of air. "I believe that's the first meal I've completed without a potty break or diaper change in forever. Don't get me wrong. I miss my kiddos, but David and I haven't had a trip alone since the kids were born." Macy glanced quickly to see Claire's reaction.

"Well, I am glad y'all could come," Claire said without missing a beat.

Claire saw the expression pass on Macy's face. It still hurt when people talked about their kids, and she imagined she would always feel some hurt, but the Lord had healed her heart, for the most part, and she didn't get angry when others spoke of their children.

Claire pushed any sadness away and let her thoughts linger on the hopes of her ovulation. She was secretly excited because she knew she and Jack had made love during her ovulation time, and she really hoped she might become pregnant again. She had not told Jack about her ovulation and wasn't sure she wanted to even mention it. She wanted to wait and see what could come to fruition.

Macy stared at Claire and could see the wheels turning. "Gentlemen, Claire, anyone want to go for a walk on the beach before we head back to our rooms?"

David and Jack nodded in agreement. They motioned for the waiter to bring the check.

As they finalized the bill, Macy leaned over to Claire. "So, you and I have something to discuss. I saw your brain working a few minutes ago."

"Shhhh. I'll tell you in a little bit." Claire looked to see if Jack had noticed.

They exited the restaurant and headed down to the beach area. Jack took Claire's hand and swung it. "David, what is your sermon about next week?"

Macy took the opportunity to steal Claire from Jack, and they lagged behind in their walk. "Go on now. Do tell."

Claire laughed at her friend as she bent down to take her sandals off. Although they didn't grow up together, Macy seemed to know her almost better than her family. "I haven't told Jack yet, so you can't say a word to David or him. Understood?"

Macy made an x over her heart. "Cross my heart."

"I'm ovulating."

"As in baby ovulating?"

"Seriously Macy, you have three children; you have to know what ovulation is."

"Of course, I do, lovey. But I wanted to hear it again," Macy said with a smile.

Claire blew out a breath of air. "You are crazy half the time. You know that right?"

"Stop the diversion and spill the beans. Tell me again." Macy clamped her hands into a please symbol.

"Okay. Macy, I'm ovulating." Claire laughed as Macy's eyes beamed with excitement.

"Which means you're thinking of trying possibly?"

"Technically, it means we could possibly be pregnant."

"What? Y'all had sex?"

Claire kicked sand lightly. "Yes, but Jack doesn't know yet."

"You had sex without Jack knowing it? Was he asleep?"

Claire laughed. "Ha. You're so funny. No, I didn't tell him I was ovulating."

Macy smiled. "I was kidding. Seriously, though, why haven't you told him? He would be stoked."

"I'm afraid that if I end up pregnant . . . well, what if I have another miscarriage? And seriously, before, it took us two years with tons of work to become pregnant. It couldn't possibly be this easy this time. I don't want to get his hope up, but I can't help but be hopeful."

"Seriously, did you just say it couldn't be possible?" Macy shook her head in disbelief. "Honey, Jesus performs miracles, and just because you had a miscarriage doesn't mean it'll happen again. Now let's get back to the real question. So y'all really did it?"

Claire laughed. "Seriously, did we do it? You sound like a teenager."

"Well, gah. I can't help it. I know y'all had a rough patch, and you said y'all hadn't done it in a while, so I'm just excited for you."

"Yeah, but we're back being 'active,' as you may say. And it has been so good."

"Well, God wants us to enjoy sex with our spouses. You've read *Song of Songs*. That's the hottest book in the Bible.

"Macy! You're a preacher's wife."

"I know, and there's nothing wrong with talking about good sex between a man and wife. I'm telling you. That's the way God planned it. So, tell me. How good was it?"

"It was amazing . . . biblical," Claire said, and she laughed as her face reddened.

"Woo-hoo," Macy yelled.

Claire laughed.

Both David and Jack turned to look at them. "What's so exciting?" David asked his wife.

The women looked at each other and busted out laughing. "Nothing," they responded in unison. The men rolled their eyes and continued their conversation.

"Seriously, I'm glad y'all are back having sex. Sex is so important in marriage. And fingers crossed and plenty of praying a baby will be made," Macy said more quietly.

"Do you think it really could happen so quickly? In all seriousness, I'm scared, Macy. What if it happens again? Or what if I can't get pregnant again?"

Macy squeezed her hand. "Honey, God's plan is already in work. Trust in Him, and with that trust comes the ability to conquer fears. Deuteronomy 31:8 says, 'He will never leave you nor forsake you. Do not be afraid, do not be discouraged.' Trust in him, Claire."

"I do trust in Him, Macy. I just don't want to face the hurt of another miscarriage. I want to be a momma so bad."

They continued walking for the next hour before heading to their rooms. When they returned to the hotel,

118 | AMANDA UMPRESS

each said their goodnights. Macy winked at Claire, and Claire blushed lightly. Jack watched the interaction with intrigue.

As Jack entered the room, he turned and looked at Claire. "So, what was the in-depth conversation tonight about between you and Macy?"

Claire studied her husband and held an inner debate. Suddenly, she blurted out, "I'm ovulating Jack."

"Ovulating huh?" Jack's face was blank of expression. "Whoa. How'd you know?"

"I kept some of the ovulation strips from when we were trying before."

"Well, you were obviously thinking about trying again. *And* you were obviously confident that you'd be getting some this week." A mischievous smile crossed Jack's face.

"Shut up," she said with a laugh. "No, of course, I want another baby."

"Well, we haven't prevented anything this week."

She bit her lip again in nervousness. "I'm not going to lie, Jack. I am terrified. What if . . ."

"No, what-ifs, BayBay. We don't play that game. We trust blindly, and we will take whatever God's plan is for us. Understand?" Her eyes met his. He held his hand out to her, and she took it. He pulled her close. "Claire, I want to make a baby with you again."

She nodded.

He picked her up and took her to the bed.

CHAPTER NINETEEN

AS SHE LAY IN THE BED, SHE COULD hear Jack in the bathroom getting ready. She couldn't believe seven weeks had passed since she and Jack were in Tampa. She had teased him that they could move there, but they both knew that would never happen. She stretched her arms out above her head, and a sudden wave of nausea hit her. She swallowed to stem the nausea, but that didn't seem to help. She jumped out of the bed and sprinted toward the bedroom.

"Hey BayBay, what's going on?" Jack asked as she streaked to the toilet. He heard the vomit and asked, "Babe, you alright?"

She wiped her mouth and sat back on the floor. "Yep, I think it's the sushi we had last night. Maybe a touch of food poisoning."

He leaned on the door frame looking at her. "I feel fine. Maybe you picked up a stomach virus in one of your offices?"

"Ugh, that's very possible since school is in session."

She puffed her cheeks out, and the nausea took force. She held up a finger and leaned over the toilet. Jack turned his head to look away.

"BayBay I'm going to go get you a cup of water. Be right back."

Claire didn't acknowledge him. After the vomiting subsided, she stood up and went to the sink. She washed her hands and splashed water onto her face. She stared at her reflection in the mirror. Her complexion was pale, and she had circles under her eyes. Suddenly, it hit her.

"I'm late," she said aloud. She stared in shock. "It couldn't be. Surely, it couldn't be." Claire turned to look at Jack as he entered the bathroom.

"You look like you've seen a ghost. You feel that bad?"

She couldn't speak. She took the glass of water and drank. As the cool water slid down her throat, an excitement bubbled into her belly.

"I feel better now."

"Good. You still look pale, though."

Debating on whether to tell Jack she was late, she stared at him with her eyes wide.

"Are you sure you're okay? You really look odd," he said cautiously.

"Jack, remember when we were in Tampa and I told you I was ovulating?"

"Yeah, why?"

"I've been so busy with work the past few weeks I didn't even realize I missed my period." She covered her mouth with her hand.

His jaw dropped open, "Seriously? You're late? Is that why you threw up? You weren't ever sick before."

"Well, Macy said that every pregnancy is different. I mean . . ."

"No way. Come on, Claire. Don't be teasing right now."

She nodded. "I wouldn't joke about this, Jack. Oh, my goodness. Oh, my goodness," she said. Then she paused. "Wait. Let's not get too excited. I haven't taken a test yet." She bit her bottom lip.

"Are you having any other pregnancy symptoms?" he asked.

She thought for a minute and then smiled slowly. "Actually, my boobs *are* sore."

"That's good. Right?"

"Good?" She laughed.

"You know what I mean. Anything else?" he asked.

She took a deep breath and thought. Her pants seemed snugger, but other than that, nothing. "Not really. Nausea and the sore breasts."

Jack nodded. "Okay, let's get in the car and go buy some pregnancy tests. We're going to the pharmacy now," he said hastily.

"Jack, we both have jobs to do today."

"Oh, crap. Yep, we do. Vacation day, maybe?"

He was nervous; she could tell. "We could do that," she said. "And maybe grab a movie as well?"

"Totally." His smile was so bright, it made her heart skip a beat.

"If the test is negative, we won't be sad. Right?" Claire watched for a reaction.

"Agreed," Jack said. "I mean we weren't seriously trying. It would be a complete miracle if you are, though."

She nodded her head and headed into their bedroom to dress. Fifteen minutes later, they stood in front of the pregnancy test aisle inside the local store. There were so many different brand choices, and Claire knew her favorites. She scanned the shelf, and all the same brands were still present.

Her phone beeped with an incoming text. She didn't bother to look at her phone. She turned her attention back to the multitude of pregnancy tests. She grabbed one from the shelf and turned it to the back to read the directions.

"Which one?" Jack looked at her with nervous eyes.

"Maybe we shouldn't get one right now. What if . . ." She placed the test back on the shelf.

"Seriously, don't go there. We're definitely getting one. Maybe twenty. However many we need to be sure."

"But what if I'm not, and what if we have another miscarriage? Jack, I'm scared."

He took her hands into his and saw the fear in her eyes. He had always been a levelheaded person, but now his hands were clammy. The same thoughts had crossed his mind. "Jesus has this, BayBay."

She nodded and grabbed three different brands of pregnancy tests. "This should be plenty don't you think?"

"Absolutely." He yanked four more from the shelf. "Maybe these, too." Jack laughed, and he leaned down to kiss Claire while holding their stash of pregnancy tests.

As they checked out, she watched the cashier place each test into the plastic bag., and her stomach flip-flopped. It had been over five months since her miscarriage, and she couldn't believe that she might be pregnant. She and Jack held hands as they walked quietly back to the car.

He opened the car door for Claire. "My Lady."

She giggled at his gesture and slid into the seat. As she waited for him to enter the car, she placed her hand gently over her abdomen. "Dear Lord, if I am, please grant me a safe pregnancy."

"You buckled up?"

"Yes. Let's head home and get this party started."

Jack laughed and cranked the car. As they drove, they chatted about their April Paris trip.

"Jack, I just thought of something."

"What is it BayBay?"

"If I'm pregnant, that would put my due date . . ." She calculated in her head the possible due date. "Mid-April or May. My due date would be around the Pinnacle Trip, and that means we wouldn't be able to go to Paris." She took a sip of her water.

Jack shrugged his shoulders. "Paris versus a baby. Which one's cheaper?"

Claire laughed loudly and slapped his shoulder gently. "The trip is free." They both laughed. "No seriously, Jack. Really."

"Okay. Okay. So what? Paris is nothing compared to us having a baby. And just think. We could take our little runt to Paris someday."

"Runt? You are full of uniqueness today." She laughed.

"I'm always full of uniqueness; that's why you married me." He winked at her and pulled into the garage.

Claire bounded out of the car quickly and slammed the car door with a thud.

"Hey, wait for me," he called as she entered the mudroom.

"You better hurry it up. I have to pee!" She raced down the hallway to the guest bathroom. As she reached the bathroom, she tore open the pregnancy kit and stared at the pregnancy test stick. "Oh, dear." She let out a puff of air as butterflies filled her stomach. "Could this really be happening right now?" Claire took three tests into the potty room and peed on each one. As she excited the bathroom, she saw Jack pacing. "Alexa, set a timer for four minutes," she called out.

"So?" Jack looked nervously at her and popped his knuckles back and forth.

"So, we wait. Four minutes."

Jack nodded. "Okay. Four long minutes. I can do this."

They paced the bedroom without words. Claire thought about their first pregnancy and how different this time would be if she was pregnant. The first pregnancy was planned, and the strategical approach was intense. She and Jack had tried to conceive for almost two years with no success. The whole process became planned; when they would have sex, what position they would have sex in, what time of the day they would have sex, depending on when Claire was most fertile. The process of conception became routine and automatic for their relationship. However, here they were now with no plan and no pressure to conceive.

The four-minute wait seemed to continue for an eternity. When the Alexa timer rang out, they stalled in their steps.

"Jack?" Claire looked for reassurance.

"Together, BayBay. Always together." He took Claire's hand. They made their way to the bathroom door. Once they were in front of the door, they took a deep breath. "Go ahead. I'll stand right here." Jack gave her a gentle nudge forward.

Claire froze. She couldn't take another step, and panic crawled up the back of her neck. "Jack, I'm scared."

"BayBay, either way, it is okay. If you're not, we can start trying. If you are, then we'll celebrate."

She blew out air and looked onto the toilet top. All the tests had turned, and she felt the tears begin to flow. She turned to look at Jack.

"Oh honey, it's okay. We can start trying."

She shook her head. "No, Jack." She took a breath and steadied herself.

"It's okay, BayBay. Don't cry. We can start trying this month. No worries, love."

She wiped away the tears and looked directly into his eyes. "Jack, I'm pregnant."

"What! Did you just say you're pregnant?" He picked her up and swirled her around. "You're pregnant? A baby? Seriously?"

She laughed and nodded her head. "Seriously, Jack. You're squeezing me too hard."

"Oops. Sorry." He kissed her lips, and he let her feet touch the floor. His hand moved to the center of her abdomen. He patted it gently as he leaned down. "Hey there, little one. I'm your daddy."

Claire's heart burst with joy as she watched her husband's reaction. "Jack you're going to be an amazing father. I love you so much." She kissed him again. In the back of her mind, a small fear lurked with what-ifs, but for now, she pushed them back.

"And you're going to rock mommy hood! So how far along do you think you are?"

She pressed her lips together to think. "I was ovulating

in Tampa, so that puts us around six weeks, give or take, with an anticipated due date of April, like I mentioned earlier."

"Our baby is six weeks old. That is amazing. God is so good."

"Jack, honey, we don't need to be so excited until we make it past twelve weeks. I . . . I just don't want us to get hurt again."

"BayBay, I love you, and I love this baby already. And God has given us a huge blessing today. I will not be shackled by fears of the past. I will rise up and shout glory to God for this little one."

She smiled at her husband's earnest love. He gave love without any constraint, and she loved this most about him. She didn't want to squash his excitement, but she knew the possibility was great that she may not be able to carry the baby.

"Okay, Jack. You can shout from the rooftops. But can we please not tell our family until the doctor thinks we are safe?"

"Sure, but as soon as he says we're good, I'm putting it on billboards all across the county." He was exploding with excitement.

Claire nodded her head in agreement. "Want to grab some breakfast now? I'm starving."

"Oh, I completely forgot we hadn't eaten. You need to feed that baby of mine. Want to go out for breakfast or stay in?"

"Let's go to Cracker Barrel. I'm craving their pancakes."

"Let the cravings begin. Wooohooo. BayBay, we are pregnant!"

CHAPTER TWENTY

CLAIRE LAID HER HAND ON TOP OF her bulging belly. She felt a kick and smiled. She took a deep breath and closed her eyes to take in the moment. Her child was due any time. The season of April in Tennessee brought flowers in full bloom, fresh green grass, birds singing, and an abundance of sunshine. She smiled, thinking about the day ahead of her. Today wasn't just any Sunday. No, it was Easter Sunday—the day she would go back to church.

Claire had resisted attending Church until she felt her baby was safe from miscarriage. Though she felt her faith return, she still had apprehensions about going back to the place where her miscarriage began. At nine months pregnant, she knew the baby was safe, and realistically, Claire knew she should have been in church months ago. But today, something brewed within her spirit—an urgency to attend worship and be in God's house. She knew God was convicting her, and she no longer could turn her back on His convictions.

She waddled into the kitchen as Jack made breakfast. Hearing her enter, Jack turned, and she saw the shock on his face, seeing her wearing a dress. He waited until she spoke.

"Jack, Happy Easter."

"Happy, Happy Easter, BayBay. You sure do look beautiful this morning." He leaned over and kissed her.

"I'm ready to go to church today," she said softly. "It's time."

"Are you sure?" he asked gently. "It's been a while."

She laughed gently. "A while?"

"Okay, more like twelve months, but who's counting," he teased. "How are you feeling? How's my itty bitty one?" He pointed toward her protruding abdomen.

"We're both good. Hungry, but good." She patted her abdomen.

"Good news then. I've made omelets. And coffee." He winked.

"Coffee, oh how I miss real coffee." She pouted.

"After itty bit comes, you can have some coffee."

"Can I at least take a whiff of it?" She laughed.

"Yes, or you can have this cup of decaf I made you." He passed her a steaming cup of coffee filled with creamer and sugar.

"Well, I guess that'll have to do." She took her coffee and made her way to the table. As she pulled her chair closer to the table, she laughed because her protruding belly limited the distance. "Look, Jack. I'm so far from the table now."

"Ha, let me get a picture." He hurried to grab his phone. "Smile big! I want itty bit to see how big momma was."

She smiled. "Excuse me. You know better than to call a woman big."

"Big, is a term of endearment." He placed her food in front of her and took his seat. "Claire, seriously, are you ready for church? You don't have to do this. I've already told you. I understand."

She picked up her fork and pushed her omelet around gently, hesitating to answer. She knew this was a shock, and he had stopped asking her to attend months ago. She was disappointed in herself for letting her fears control her ability to step into the church. Macy and David had not pressured her or even questioned her decision. In truthfulness, she avoided the conversation with Macy at all costs.

"Earth to Claire," Jack said.

"Oh, sorry. What was the question?"

"Are you sure you want to attend church today?"

Claire nodded her head and finally took a bite of her omelet.

"Okay. I'm glad you're going with me. I know it's not easy for you. And if you get overwhelmed, just let me know. We can leave. Whatever feels right for you, BayBay."

"God placed the conviction on my heart to attend. Our baby is healthy and due any moment, and I honestly don't have a reason to *not* attend, beyond fear."

"Fear is a real force, and it can be powerful. But faith is more powerful." He took a sip of his coffee. "I'm proud of you, Claire."

She nodded. "Isn't it amazing how fear can immobilize us as Christians? I mean, twelve months of not attending church. I grew up in church and was there every time the door opened. One bad thing happens, and I was incapable of going back?"

"Don't be so hard on yourself. Like I said, fear is extremely powerful. A scripture my mom read to me when I was growing up was Psalms 18:2. 'The Lord is my rock, my fortress, and my deliverer.' If your convictions are weighing heavily to attend church today, then he is delivering you from your fear."

"I'm ready, Jack. I want to start afresh with our baby, and I want him or her to experience a childhood with church as a regular part of it. And if I'm not in church, then how will I set a Godly example for them to follow?"

"I'm very proud of you," he said.

"You've already said that," she said with a smile. "But why are you proud? You tried to get me to go back for so long, and I was pretty mean to you about it."

"I'm proud because you are strong, and conquering a fear isn't easy. Yes. I've been waiting for this moment since last year, but I realized that this is something that you had to do on your time—on God's time—not on my time. And now, well, it's time. I Love you, BayBay, and I'll be right by your side today and every day."

"I love you, and I know Jesus put you in my life to be my sidekick." She paused. "Now enough of the seriousness. Who's cleaning the kitchen?" She patted her stomach while batting her eyes.

He raised his hand. "I suppose it will be me." He laughed and began to clear the table. "Hey, don't forget your parents, your brothers, and your sister will be here this afternoon for lunch and the Easter egg hunt. David and Macy and the kids are coming too."

"Oh, that's right. I can't believe I almost forgot. Mom hasn't called yet, which is strange." As she finished her sentence, the phone rang.

"Momma Beth?" Jack asked, looking at the phone.

Claire examined the caller ID. "Yep. I'm going to take the call while I finish getting ready." She kissed Jack and walked to the bathroom.

CHAPTER TWENTY-ONE

JACK PULLED INTO THE CHURCH PARKING LOT and looked over to Claire. He could see the fear on her face, and he grabbed her hand. "We can leave if you want."

She shook her head and squeezed his hand. "I'm good, Jack."

He came around the car and opened her door. As she swung her legs to the side, she felt a small contraction. She placed her hand over her stomach and made a slight grimace.

"What? What's wrong?" Jack asked worriedly.

"I think it's a mild contraction."

"What? What's that mean? Are we having a baby? Should we go to the hospital?"

Claire laughed. "Nothing to worry about, Jack. On my last appointment, the doctor said that little contractions are normal." She took his hand and pushed on the door frame to stand.

"Claire!" She turned her head to the voice and smiled. Macy waved from the church steps. She walked hand in hand with Jack to Macy and David.

"Oh, Claire, you're here." Macy hugged her tightly. "I

can't believe you're here." Tears sprang from her eyes. "Stupid hormones, gets me every time."

"How is that sweet baby boy in there?" Claire patted Macy's stomach.

Claire was so excited that Macy and David were expecting their fourth child. They had already decided their children would be best friends. She was so amazed by how quickly things could change in a year.

"Gabe is just like his daddy. Feisty little thing." She smiled. "But you're here. What happened to make you attend?"

"Macy, leave her alone," David interjected. "Claire, what my wife means to say is that we are very excited to have you back." Macy elbowed him gently.

"Thank you, David. I'm glad to be back." Claire's eyes were drawn to the parking lot where she saw a familiar face. "Is that Reese?" Claire waived big and motioned for Reese to join them. "Reese, you're here?" Claire asked amazed.

"Hello, Claire. It's nice to see you again." She turned her attention to the group. "Pastor David and Macy. It is nice to see you all."

David and Jack spoke, while Claire tried to understand the scenario.

Macy hugged Reese. "Glad you are here on this glorious day. How are you feeling this morning?"

"I'm feeling good. A little tired. But overall good."

"Do you two know each other?" Claire asked.

Macy laughed and turned to Claire. "Oh dear, you don't know do you? I guess I hadn't thought to mention it."

Reese laughed and looked from Macy to Claire.

"Reese began attending our church a few months back. December or January, I believe," Macy said questionably.

"It was in December," Reese responded.

"Oh, I didn't know that," Claire said.

"Now why would you, Hun?" Macy said with a smile. "Reese is a local nurse at the hospital downtown."

Claire nodded. "Yes, Reese was my nurse when I had my miscarriage."

"Really? I guess I didn't link the connection. I'm sorry," Macy responded.

Reese smiled and nodded. "Yes, I was Claire's nurse." She looked to Jack to see if he recognized her.

"Hi, again," Jack said. "I didn't realize it either. I've seen you at church, but I didn't connect the dots either."

Reese shrugged her shoulders. "No worries."

"Wow, what a coincidence this is," Claire said.

"Yes, the small world Nashville is," Macy responded.

"Well, it's about that time," David chimed in. "Shall we?" he asked, pointing to the doors.

The Church bell rang out to signal that the morning service was to begin. "Claire?" Jack held his hand out, and she took it.

Claire engulfed a breath of air and took one step at a time up to the church doors. Macy, David, and Reese followed behind them. As Claire reached the doors, she froze. Jack stopped and waited for her next move. David excused himself and made his way to the pulpit.

"Claire, do you want to go home?" Jack asked.

"Claire, it's okay if you don't want to go in. Today was the first step. Baby steps." Macy smiled lovingly.

Reese stood to the side to give Claire some breathing room.

Claire closed her eyes for a moment and silently prayed. *Dear Lord, give me the strength to overcome my fear.* Then, she opened her eyes and looked at her husband and best friend, so graceful, telling her it'd be okay for her to go home. Tears sprang to her eyes.

"Y'all are so sweet and understanding—and after the way I treated you about this. I'm so blessed to have you both."

Jack smiled, and Macy said, "I love you, honey."

Claire smiled. "Okay. I'm ready." She took another step. Jack squeezed her hand gently in support. As she entered the lobby, she heard the choir's voices. Several congregation members stared at her but made no motion to speak. As she followed Jack, Macy, and Reese, the miscarriage replayed in her mind.

She shook her head. "Not today Satan, not today. I am free from the anger. I am free from the fear."

"Claire, did you say something?" Macy asked.

"No, I'm good."

"Where do you want to sit?" Jack looked toward the pews in the Chapel.

"Anywhere is fine. Reese, would you like to sit with us?" Claire asked.

"Yes, please."

She motioned for Reese to slide into the pew behind Macy, and once seated, Claire picked up her hymnal. For the first time in twelve months, she joined in as the choir sang out on this Easter Sunday.

CHAPTER TWENTY-TWO

CLAIRE WAS THANKFUL FOR THE LOVE AND support of her family. She survived her first church service since her miscarriage and now no longer doubted God's relentless love for her. She knew that her own hurt had delayed her return, and Claire felt embarrassed of the way she had acted for the past year, but she was thankful that her family and friends had forgiven her.

Claire smiled as she heard the laughter from her family enjoying their Easter afternoon. *Next year, our baby will be able to hunt Easter eggs,* she thought. "Thank you, Jesus, for this child. Thank you, Jesus, for giving me the strength to go to church again, and thank you, Jesus, for loving me wholeheartedly," she whispered as she rubbed her belly.

Claire's family had arrived earlier to prepare for Easter; her brothers had stashed the Easter eggs across the lawn for Emma, Lucy, and Amber. She saw Gabby's reflection out of the corner of her eye and readjusted in her seat to watch. Gabby was helping Lucy who had just found three eggs behind the tree in the corner. She laughed at her sister's awkwardness with the little girl. Gabby was many things, but a fan of small children, she was not. She had no desire to be a parent herself. Claire laughed because she knew someday that would change for her sister—especially when she found the love of her life, which reminded Claire to ask her how her date went Friday night with Chad Taylor, the junior partner from Jack's firm.

Gabby's eyes met Claire's. "We need to talk about Chad," Claire mouthed.

Rolling her eyes, Gabby mouthed, "You are so nosey!"

Laughing, Claire's attention turned to Macy. She looked radiant with her blonde curly hair flowing past her shoulders and her little baby bump. She held Amber's hand to steady the toddler as she bent down near the pool to find a golden egg. Amber picked up the egg, and with excitement, she looked over at Claire and waved.

"Great find, Amber," Claire called out.

Claire shifted as the baby moved and plastered a foot into her stomach.

"Hey, sis."

Claire turned to see the twins exiting the house. "Hey guys, you didn't want to Easter egg hunt?" She laughed.

"Seriously?" Ezra rolled his eyes.

"Claire, if it's a boy, you know we'll teach him to play football," Francis commented.

"What if it's a girl?" she asked.

"Oooh, we don't need any other girls. We need some testosterone in this family." Ezra made a crinkled face.

"Girls can play football, too," Francis said elbowing his twin.

Claire laughed at her brothers. They were eighteen and graduating high school in less than one month. "Have y'all decided which college offer you'll accept?" She couldn't believe her baby brothers were headed to college. Francis had been offered an academic scholarship to an Ivy League school and an in-state school. He was graduating at the top of his class. Ezra had been offered a scholarship to an in-state school to play football in Tennessee at a small, private college.

"We haven't decided. And it's driving mom crazy." Francis spoke first.

"I may not go to college." Ezra laughed and winked at his sister.

"Um. Sure. Boys, college is very important. Y'all need to decide soon before you lose your spot."

"Okay. You twisted my arm. I'll go to college—but just for the chicks." Ezra let out a loud laugh.

Claire shook her head playfully. "Seriously Ezra, when will you grow up?"

He shrugged his shoulders. "Growing up is over-rated."

Francis elbowed his brother again. "Dude, stop being stupid."

Ezra shoved Francis.

"Boys, seriously stop." Claire laughed.

They both grinned. "Sure, thing sis," Francis said. They blew her a kiss and walked away.

Claire surveyed the crowd again and saw Jack and David manning the grill. She smelled the steaks cooking and suddenly felt hungry.

"Hey Jack, hurry up over there. Me and this monstrous baby of ours are hungry."

He winked at her and shook his spatula. "Coming right up for the big pregnant lady at the table."

Claire scowled. "Better watch what you say there, mister. These hormones are no joke, and I might give you 'big' whooping."

"I told you, 'big' is a term of endearment," he yelled.

They both laughed. Claire rubbed her hand across her protruding belly. She still couldn't believe she had made it this far into her pregnancy. Her due date of April tenth was fast approaching. At her doctor's visit on Friday, he warned her to be prepared for the baby's arrival at any time. She and Jack had been super busy in the past few months getting the nursery ready. David, Macy, and her family had all chipped in with the painting and massive amounts of putting furniture together. Since she and Jack had chosen not to find out the gender, they went with neutral colors. They painted the nursery grey with highlights of silver and gold. It was stunning. She had three baby showers, and each produced more than enough items for their child. Her mother was the ringleader of buying baby items. As Beth would say, "It's a grandmother's duty to spoil her grandchild rotten."

She was driving Macy and her mother crazy because they hadn't agreed on a baby name yet. Everyone had opinions on names—especially her mother. Beth wanted the baby's name to be Louise after her mother. Jack fiercely shot that name down and claimed if it was a boy, he wanted the name to be Hudson George. Jack told everyone that it was a strong attorney name and that he knew his son would follow his example. Gabby broke his heart when she reminded him that Baby St. John might just happen to be a girl.

Claire's thoughts were interrupted by the feeling of something trickling down her leg. She shifted in the patio chair to adjust, and she peered over her massive belly, only seeing clear liquid.

"Either I peed in my pants, or the baby is coming!" she shouted louder than she initially intended.

Heads turned, and everyone sprinted toward her.

"It's time?" Jack asked in a panicked voice.

Claire nodded as a contraction surged. She grimaced.

"Breathe, Breathe. Was that a contraction?" Jack asked.

"Honey, where is your bag? Momma'll grab it for you," Beth said.

"Here comes the baby," Ezra yelled.

"Woo-hoo," Francis roared.

"Does it hurt?" Gabby asked.

"Yep. Her water definitely broke," Ezra said.

"I'm so excited," Macy screamed.

"What's going on?" David asked, ambling toward them.

"Everybody shut up," Claire yelled.

Everyone grew silent.

Then, Claire started laughing. "I'm sorry," she said through giggles. "Yes. I'm having contractions. Oh, it hurts!!! HHHHHH," she hissed through teeth.

"Time them, Mica. Don't just stand there. Good grief you're a doctor," Beth yelled.

"Beth, I'm not an OBGYN. And that's my baby girl," Mica shouted back.

"I can time them," Macy said calmly. "Everyone, take a deep breath and get it together please." Macy smiled.

"Hhhhhhhh. Owwww." Claire blew out a breath.

"Come on Claire. Take my hand; we have you." Jack took one hand, and Mica grabbed the other.

"They're about five minutes apart," Macy called while she followed them.

"In my room by the door. HHHH . . . Owwww. It hurts. The bag is by my door," she screamed. "Oh . . . HHHHH." She breathed through contractions.

"Gabby can you grab the kids and take them inside please?" Macy called out from over her shoulder.

"Of course." Gabby nodded. "I love you, sis!"

"Me . . . HHHH . . . too," she said between breaths.

Beth, Mica, Macy, David, and the twins followed her and Jack into the garage. One of the twins opened the car door as Beth put a towel down to protect the seats. Claire slid into the seat and closed her eyes as another contraction took hold.

"Is the car seat ready?" Beth asked.

"Yeah. I stopped by the fire station, and they made sure it was done correctly." Jack fidgeted with his keys and dropped them. "Shoot." He leaned down to pick them up.

"Breathe, Jack. We need you to stay calm," Mica spoke sternly and calmly.

Jack nodded and slid into the car. "Yes, sir. I've got this." He closed the car door as Claire made panting sounds.

"Owwwwwww. Another one is happening." Claire grabbed the dash as the contraction clinched her abdomen.

"Breathe, honey. Breathe." Beth blew Claire a kiss and closed the car door.

Jack lowered the car windows and began to back up out of the garage "We're going to have a baby!" he yelled excitedly.

"Yes, you are!" David yelled.

"We'll follow you," Beth called out as they peeled out of the driveway.

Claire waved out the car window as Jack sped down their neighborhood drive. "Jack, you may need to slow down." Claire looked over at her husband, and his face was focused on the road.

"Okay, BayBay. Just hold on. I'll get us there." He placed the hazard lights on as he entered the on-ramp for the interstate. He switched in and out of lanes as needed. She felt the contractions increase, and her breathing techniques continued. By her calculation, her contractions were getting shorter and shorter.

They made it to the hospital in record time, and Claire's heart skipped a beat. Jack quickly pulled into a parking spot near the emergency room and jumped out of his seat.

"Jack, the car's still running."

"Oh, yeah. Sorry!"

"Breathe, Jack. Breathe. We're about to have a baby," Claire said assuredly. As he rounded the front of the car to her door, realization set in. The last time she was there, she had her miscarriage. She closed her eyes and prayed. "Dear Lord, you are amazing and have blessed us with this child. As a new mother, I'm scared. I ask that the birth goes easily without complications and that our child is healthy. In your name, Amen." She opened her eyes as Jack was opening her door.

"You okay?"

Claire nodded her head. He reached his hand out, and she took it. He pulled gently to help her get up, and she wobbled as the weight of the baby balanced. "Jack, I can't believe it is time. We get to meet our child soon."

"God is good, BayBay. God is good."

"All the time. Are you ready to be a daddy?"

"As ready as I can be. I'm nervous and excited."

"Me too. I can't believe it's time." She grimaced as a contraction hit.

"It's crazy how fast the past few months have gone by. I want to be the best daddy to our baby, and I promise I'll do everything within my power to be. I love you Claire, and I love this child of ours."

"Me too. HHHHHH . . . And I love you, too. Now, shut up and get me in there." She exhaled loudly.

As they entered the hospital hand in hand, they knew their life would change forever.

CHAPTER TWENTY-THREE

"It's time to start pushing, Claire. You're fully dilated to ten centimeters," Dr. Cook said gently. "When I count to three, I want you to push. Ready?"

Claire blew out a breath of air and nodded. "Yes. Owwww. It's so painful."

"Is it too late to get her that epidural?" Jack asked concerned.

"I'm sorry Mr. St. John; it is. She is past the point of . . ."

Claire's scream interrupted his sentence. She squeezed Jack's hand and waited for the contraction to finish.

"Okay, Claire. It's time. On my count."

She nodded and looked to Jack.

"1 . . . 2 . . . 3 . . . Push, Claire."

"AHHHHH," Claire screamed as she pushed. Her face squinted and sweat beaded on her head. She gritted her teeth as the pressure intensified.

"Great job, Claire. Now take a deep breath." He studied her for a moment. "Claire, I can see the baby's head. And a head full of hair."

"What, my baby has hair?" She cried as the hormones, love, and pain consumed her.

"Alright, Claire. Let's do this again," Dr. Cook instructed.

She held Jack's hand so tightly, her knuckles were white. "I can't. It hurts so bad. I'm exhausted."

"Come on, BayBay. You've got this. Push honey. You're strong," Jack said as his breath quickened.

Claire glared at Jack. "It hurts!"

Jack knew better than to comment. David had warned him her personality might change during the birthing process. Claire had been very insistent to have the baby naturally, yet now, he wished he had pressed her to have the epidural. Maybe if she had opted to have the epidural, she wouldn't be in such pain.

"Claire, it's time to push. There is no other option. Do you understand me?" Dr. Cook looked firmly at her. "On the count of three, push with all your might."

Claire nodded as she pursed her lips and started another breathing technique. The nurse handed Jack a cup of ice and a cold cloth. Jack placed the cloth on her forehead as the doctor turned his attention back to the baby.

"1 . . . 2 . . . 3 . . . Push Claire, Push!"

"Ahhhhhhh. Ohhhhhhh. Ahhhhhhh! Oh, my goodness! Jack! Help me. It hurts so bad! AHHHHHHHHHHH . . ."

"Waah . . . Waah . . . Waah."

The sounds filled the delivery room. In an instant, Claire's pain and suffering vanished, replaced by love. She and Jack looked at each other as the sounds of their child filled the room. Tears of joy filled their eyes. They looked toward Dr. Cook as he held up their child. For the first time, at three-forty-five in the afternoon, Jack and Claire saw their child.

"Congratulations, Claire and Jack. You have a healthy baby girl," Dr. Cook said with pride.

"A girl?" Claire and Jack asked simultaneously.

Jack's eyes were full of tears, and they spilled down his cheek as his dark-headed daughter cried. The doctor passed her to the nurse, and his attention went to the umbilical cord.

"She's beautiful."

"Oh Jack, look at her. Look at our daughter." Claire closed her eyes and lifted her head toward the ceiling. "Oh, thank you, Jesus. Oh, thank you." Tears of joy flowed down her face, and she felt love like she had never known. She was finally a mother.

"Jack, do you want to cut the cord?" Dr. Cook asked.

Jack looked at Claire with a slight nervousness, and she smiled to fill him with confidence. Jack nodded to Dr. Cook and made his way to the end of the bed. He saw the blood and felt queasy. He steadied himself as Dr. Cook passed the medical scissors to him. He hesitated slightly but snipped the cord between Claire and their daughter. The umbilical cord severed; the nurse took their daughter to clean her up. After a few newborn tests and some monitoring, the nurse rounded the side of the bed and laid the baby girl on Claire's chest.

Claire sighed. Her daughter whimpered as she felt her mother. They breathed in rhythm, and Claire leaned down, kissing her baby.

"Oh Jack, look at her."

"She's as beautiful as her mother," Jack said as he stroked Claire's hair.

"Mr. and Mrs. St. John, does baby St. John have a name?" the nurse asked.

Jack and Claire both let a giggle out and looked at each other. Claire bit her lip as Jack nodded. "Her name is Charlotte Emeline St. John," Claire said lovingly.

CHAPTER TWENTY-FOUR

ELATED WITH JOY, JACK WALKED DOWN the hall to the labor and delivery waiting room. As he entered, he saw their family there, including his parents, his older brother Nolan, and their best friends. His parents had flown in from their beach home in Jacksonville. His dad sat in the corner with Claire's dad, and his mother was chatting amiably with Beth. His heart was so happy that his parents had made it. He saw Macy and David sitting side by side near the window, holding hands. The twins and Gabby were at the table playing a hand of cards, where one of the twins was taunting the other for a failed play.

He felt blessed beyond measure, and his heart filled with excitement to announce the arrival of his precious Charlotte. As the door closed, all eyes fell upon him, and he could see their anticipation.

Beth was the first to speak. "Jack, is my grandshug here yet? How is my Claire?"

Jack looked at Beth and nodded. "Yes, the baby is here. Claire is good. Everything went well."

"Well son, come on and spit out. Is it a girl or boy?" Mica chimed in, obviously aggravated.

Jack's mother, Donna came close to her son. She touched his face gently and embraced him for a hug. She kissed his cheek, "Hi, honey."

"Hey, mom. I'm so glad y'all made it in time."

"We wouldn't have missed our grandchild's debut," Donna said lovingly.

Jack turned his attention to his father, of whom he was spitting image. "Hey, Dad."

Charles came up to his son, shook his hand, and gave him an embrace. "Hi, son. How are you holding up?"

"I'm good, dad. It's been the most amazing adventure of my life." Jack turned to his brother.

"Good to see you," Nolan said patting Jack on the shoulder.

"You too. Glad you made it here. How was your flight?"

"It was good. I took the red-eye out of London two days ago." Nolan glanced toward Donna and winked. "Mom promised to disinherit me if I missed the birth of my niece or nephew."

"Nolan St. John! You need to hush now." Donna laughed.

"Okay now. That's enough of the meet and greet. Can we please get the details on my grandshug?" Beth asked hurriedly.

Jack laughed at his mother-in-law. "Of course, Beth. I'm sorry. It's been such a rollercoaster. The baby is healthy and the most beautiful baby I have ever seen."

"Jack!" Everyone said in unison.

"Alright. Alright." He laughed and winked at his mom. "I am proud to announce on behalf of Claire and myself that we have a beautiful . . ."

Gabby rolled her eyes. "Seriously, Jack, would you spit it out already? You're likely to drive my mother insane."

"We have a very beautiful and amazingly healthy baby girl."

"A girl!" Beth covered her mouth with her hand. She and Donna hugged while Gaby and Macy jumped up and down as cheers, pats on the back, high-fives, and celebratory movements flowed through the waiting room.

Jack waited for the celebration to get quiet. "She weighed in at seven pounds and three ounces. She measured twenty-one inches long. Her feet and hands are so tiny."

"Oh my, she sounds darling." Donna's eyes were full of emotion as she watched her son talk about his own child.

"Good grief, Jack. Does my grandshug have a name at least?" Beth asked.

Jack laughed slightly as he realized he had forgotten to mention the baby's name. "Yes, sorry. Of course. We've named her Charlotte Emeline St. John. We want to call her Emmie." He beamed with pride as he said his daughter's name.

Beth and Donna placed their hands over their chest. Macy had tears in her eyes as she looked toward Jack.

"Oh, Jack, that's beautiful," Macy claimed.

"Mighty fine name, Jack," Mica stated.

Charles patted his son on the back. "How's it feel to be a dad, son?"

Jack realized that the moment Charlotte Emeline entered the world, his whole life changed. It was a love like no other for him.

"Jack?"

"Sorry, Dad. I'm in a whirlwind I suppose."

"Jack what does she look like?" Beth asked, and Donna nodded.

"She came out with a head full of black hair, and she's the most beautiful baby in the whole world." He laughed gently. "She has Claire's nose and my eyes. She has lungs like you wouldn't believe. With lungs like I witnessed this afternoon, I just know she'll follow in her daddy's footsteps."

"Dude, you're a dad. How weird is that?" Ezra patted Jack on the back.

"That's not strange, stupid. It is the evolution of life. Man meets woman; man and woman produce a baby. Geeze, Ezra I worry about you." Francis rolled his eyes at his brother.

"Smart boys." Nolan laughed.

Donna sent Nolan a sideways glance, "Jack, may we see Emmie and Claire?" She asked kindly.

He nodded. "Yes, mom. Let me go back and check to see when y'all can visit. I'll text one of you when it's good to come back."

"My phone is charged fully, Jack." Beth held her phone up.

He hugged his mom and waved to them as he headed out the doors. "It shouldn't be long; I promise."

As he walked down the corridor, his mind reeled with the events of the day. He was a daddy. A daddy. His mind couldn't grasp the concept yet. He looked through the window of the nursery and didn't see Emmie. He made his way to Claire's room, and as he entered, he stopped dead in his tracks. There was his wife and child. Claire had never looked so beautiful as she did at that moment, and his heart skipped a beat with love. Emmie was nestled on her mother's breast, eating her first meal, and Claire looked as though she had been breastfeeding their daughter forever.

Claire looked up and saw Jack watching them. She held out her right hand and motioned for him to come closer. As he came to the side of the bed, Claire patted the side for him to sit.

"Charlotte Emeline, say hi to your daddy," Claire said in a cooing voice.

"Hello, baby girl. I'm your daddy." He leaned over and kissed Emmie on her head. "I think baby girl is more worried about milk than her daddy." He laughed gently. "Emmie, daddy loves you," Jack cooed.

"I think you're correct. Isn't she amazing, Jack? Can you believe she is ours?" Claire stared into Emmie's face and was elated with joy. As she looked at her daughter, she thought of her first child. She wondered if their baby would have been a girl or boy.

"Claire. We have a beautiful daughter." Jack looked at Claire and wondered where her mind was. "Hey, you okay?" he asked.

Claire blinked away the thoughts. "Yes, sorry I was lost in my own thoughts." Claire looked down at Emmie and saw milk spill over her lips. She silently vowed to protect and love her at all costs.

"Claire, our family is dying to meet Miss Emmie," he said with a wink.

"Oh, oops I forgot. Is that terrible of me, Jack, not wanting to share this moment?"

"Not at all BayBay, but your mother has threatened to raid the labor and delivery unit to find her grandshug, and you if I don't let them in soon . . ."

Claire laughed. "I have no doubt she would too." She looked down at Emmie and saw that she has finished nursing. She laid her over her shoulder and gently patted her back.

"BayBay, you're a natural."

"Awe, thank you, love." They both smiled as a small burp erupted from baby Emmie. "You better get our family in here."

Jack nodded and sent a text to Beth. A few moments later, they heard their family's laughter carrying down the hall. Claire situated Emmie high in the crook of her arm so when they entered, they could see her beautiful daughter. "Are you ready to meet your family, my sweet Emmie?" She was fast asleep in Claire's arms, and she held her fist tightly clinched. Claire looked up to see the door open, and Beth and Donna were the first to enter.

At the sight of her own mother, Claire began to cry. "Momma, I'm so glad you're here."

"Oh, sweet Claire, you look beautiful."

Beth rounded to the side of the bed, leaned down, and kissed Claire's forehead. She then turned her attention to Emmie where she kissed her gently on the top of her head.

Claire readjusted Emmie slightly so everyone could get a better view. "Oh Donna, it's so good to see you."

"You as well, Claire. You look absolutely stunning. Are you sure you just gave birth?" Donna winked at Claire.

"Trust me; if it wasn't for this waterproof makeup, I would look a hot mess." She looked down at Emmie. "But she is worth anything. Everyone, please meet Charlotte Emeline St. John, our Easter baby."

In a chorus-like sound, the entire room cooed at the

baby. Beth placed one hand over her heart and one over her mouth. Mica looked at his daughter and granddaughter, astonished his firstborn was a mother. The baby mesmerized the twins. Gabby moved in closer to get a better view and drew in her breath at the sight of her niece.

"Emmie, please meet your grandparents, aunt, and uncles. And your God-parents."

Macy and David exchanged looks of surprise. "Godparents? Us?" Macy asked.

"Yes, you," Claire responded.

Macy couldn't hold the tears of joy back. She nodded and tried to speak. "Claire, Jack, oh what an amazing honor you do us."

Beth couldn't stand it any longer. She held out her arms to Emmie. "Claire, hand her over to me right this instant." Claire shifted Emmie gently in a means to pass her to Beth. As Beth took Emmie, she cooed at her. "Hello, Emmie. I am grandmama, and you're my grandshug. I may just possibly call you shug." Beth continued to cuddle the infant.

"Grandmama?" Ezra asked. "Seriously mom that makes you sound like you're ancient."

"Agreed," Francis chimed in.

"I'll have you know that grandmomma is what I called my grandmother. Humph." Emmie stirred in Beth's arms. "So, what do you believe is an appropriate name for Emmie to call me?"

"I, for one, would like to be called grandmother," Donna chimed in. "Is that acceptable, boys, for someone of my age?" Donna raised an eyebrow to the boys.

Beth gently passed the infant to Donna, and Emmie awoke during the transfer. She let out a little wail that

Donna silenced by the slow sway of her arms. "Shhh, little one. Grandmother has you."

"Well, mother, I think meme or nana would be more suitable." Francis elbowed his brother for support.

"Yep, I agree." Ezra looked annoyingly at his brother.

"Claire, what do you like the best, lovely?" Beth waited for a response from Claire.

"Well, mom I personally like both of the boys' suggestions. And to be honest, I am *not* a fan of grandshug." Claire grimaced as she spoke the truth.

Jack and David both muffled laughs. "Claire, tread lightly sweetheart," Mica said jokingly.

Beth shot all three men a look that would frighten anyone. "I swear, you three. Okay, let me think on it. I don't believe Emmie needs an answer today, anyway."

"Of course not, mom," Claire responded as her attention turned to Emmie who was crying again. "She's probably hungry again. Boys, do y'all mind giving me a moment to feed her?" Before she even had the words out completely, the men had cleared the room. She pulled her gown down and placed Emmie gently on her breast. .

"Claire, you're a natural," Macy said lovingly.

"Macy, I remembered all your tricks from your breastfeeding days. And to speak of breastfeeding, how are you feeling? How is the baby?" Claire nodded toward Macy's stomach.

"A baby, Oh! How exciting, Macy. I didn't even notice. I'm sorry." Donna rounded the bed to reach Macy where she gave her a hug.

"Thank you, Donna. No worries. David and I are very

excited. The girls are less enthusiastic. But what's the most exciting is that our little one and Emmie will be best friends."

"Do you know what you're having yet?"

Macy smiled at Charlotte and nodded. "We actually found out last week. We told Claire and Jack immediately."

"Oh, Macy, do tell us," Beth said excitedly.

"I really don't want to impede on Claire and Charlotte's day."

"Impede? Hogwash. Claire, honey, tell Macy to spill it." Beth snorted gently.

"Claire, you have to tell them. They won't rest until you spill the beans. Anyway, Emmie is just fine and content drinking her milk." Claire radiated with pride as she spoke.

Macy nodded at Claire and smiled. "We are having a baby boy."

"A boy!" Beth said so loudly that Charlotte de attached from nursing. Claire shifted the baby to align her again.

"Mom, a little quieter next time, please."

Beth laughed gently. "Sorry, dear. That's amazing, Macy." Beth got up from the chair and rounded the bed to hug Macy. "Do you have a named picked out yet?"

"We do, Beth. We've chosen to name the baby Gabriele David Mize. The girls like the name Gabe as his shortened name."

"That is beautiful. Just beautiful."

"Thank you, Beth."

"I second that," Claire said quietly to not disturb Charlotte. "Charlotte and Gabe will be best friends forever."

"Well, I bet Charlotte and Gabe will get married someday." Everyone turned to the door and saw Gabby still standing there. "Well, yeah, I'm still here," she said, shrugging her shoulders upward.

The ladies in the room laughed at Gabby's comment. "Let's not fast forward that much, just yet," Claire said. "I need for her to grow up just a little."

"And I still need for Gabe to make his debut." Macy laughed.

"Mark my words. Just wait and see," Gabby said with an air of arrogance.

CHAPTER TWENTY-FIVE

THE SUN BEAMED FROM THE CLEAR, blue sky. Laughter filled the air as Emmie and Gabe played in the sandbox by the patio. Claire watched her eighteen-month-old and Macy's son Gabe, who was only two months younger than Emmie. Since Gabe and Emmie's arrival, Macy and Claire had been inseparable, seeing each other daily. Gabe and Emmie had created an amazing bond, playing together for hours. When it was naptime, Macy and Claire would have to make sure they were lying next to each other on their nap mats, or Emmie would throw a fit.

"Claire, are they alright?" Macy called from the patio.

Claire held up a thumb. "Doing great if you count eating sand five thousand times." Claire laughed.

"I hear it has protein."

Claire nodded at her friend. "So, I hear. And I suppose the bugs are considered protein as well. Yuck." Claire made a yucky face for the kids.

Emmie and Gabe let out a squeal of joy as Claire crunched her face to match her words. "Illy mom," Emmie said.

Gabe pointed to Claire. "f . . . a . . . ce," Gabe stuttered.

Claire made silly faces, and the babies laughed unconditionally. Gabe picked up a handful of sand and tossed it at Emmie playfully. Emmie, startled by the sand hitting her face, began to cry, and she reached for Claire.

"No. no. no," Emmie stammered.

"It's okay, honey. Let momma dust you off." Claire picked Emmie up from the sandbox.

Macy walked up to the sandbox and kneeled. "Gabe, no-no. We don't throw sand." Macy scolded him gently. "Do you to stop playing?"

"Me pay. Me pay. No. No," he said stubbornly.

Claire tried to cover her laugh as Gabe clapped his hands together. Sand spewed in the air, and he blinked as the sand speckled his face. He crossed his arms with a pout and hung his head. Macy reached over and picked him up.

"Gabe, tell Emmie you're sorry." Macy pointed her finger toward Emmie.

"No," he said, pouting.

"Gabe Mize, you do as you're told." Macy looked sternly at him.

Gabe studied his mother's expression. "Me surry, Em."

Emmie laid her head on her Claire and looked at her friend. "Emmie, tell Gabe you forgive him, love."

Emmie hesitated to understand. "Me kay."

Claire shrugged her shoulders and shifted Emmie. "How about we go get some juice boxes?"

Both toddlers cheered in response, and all was forgotten as they walked toward the house. Claire's heart was so full of love and happiness, and the past miscarriage seemed like a lifetime ago. She still thought of her unborn child, but now, she was amazed by God's continued grace and love for her.

As they entered the French doors, she could hear Jack and David yelling at the television. Both men were perched on the edge of the couch, deeply involved in the game.

"Who's winning?" she asked.

"Dadda," Emmie squealed while holding her arms out.

"Vandy is," Jack responded. "Come over here, Emmie. Sit with daddy."

Emmie scrambled out of Claire's arms and wobbled to sit in Jack's lap. "Dadda. Me em." She squealed with excitement. When she reached Jack's lap, she held her arms up for assistance.

He reached down and picked her up. She snuggled against her daddy and began to suck her thumb.

"Emmie, we don't suck our thumb honey," Claire called out.

"Me yes," Emmie said.

"No, honey. It's not good for you." Claire looked at Jack for assistance. "Jack?"

"Emmie, no sucking that little thumb of yours. Daddy doesn't want your teeth to get crooked like a monster." He tickled her.

"Eeeh, me no mon." She giggled and wiggled in his lap.

Claire laughed and threw her hands up in defeat. She walked into the kitchen to prepare the kids a snack. She surveyed the fridge and decided on two juice boxes out of the fridge.

"Juice? And cheese puffs?" she asked Macy.

"Sure, that's fine by me."

Claire went to the pantry and settled on cheese puffs, placing them on the table.

"Perfect." Macy smiled and put Gabe in his travel booster, and she handed him a few cheese puffs.

Claire turned toward Jack and Claire. "Come on, sweetheart; it's time for your snack."

"Nak, Nak, Nak." Charlotte clapped her hands. "Me nak. Me nak."

"Me snack huh?" Jack laughed.

Emmie waddled to Claire and held her arms up. "Me nak, me nak."

"Here you go, sweetheart. Chew good, okay?" Claire tightened her safety belt.

"Hey BayBay, what do y'all want for dinner?" Jack asked from the couch.

"Macy?" Claire asked.

"How about pizza? David, how does that sound?"

David gave Macy a thumbs up. "Whatever y'all decide works for me. I'm easy to please."

"As long as he doesn't have to cook it." Macy gently elbowed Claire.

Claire giggled. "Pizza, Jack?"

"Sounds good. How about ordering it from Antonio's? David wants supreme." Jack laughed, as he knew he favored supreme more than his friend.

"Supreme works. Shoot, how did he miss that?" David asked absentmindedly.

"Okay. Supreme good for you, Macy?" Claire asked.

"Yep. Sounds good," Macy replied.

"Good deal. I'll order it. One cheese for the kids and

one supreme for us." Claire picked up the phone and placed the order. "Thirty minutes. Macy, If I go pick it up, will you watch the kids? The guys are way too involved in the game." She laughed.

"Of course. I have it under control."

"Awesome, thank you. I need to grab my keys." Claire went into the mudroom to grab her car keys when she heard Macy's cell phone ringing. She walked back into the kitchen to tell everyone goodbye as Macy was answering.

"Hello, this is Macy." She heard Macy pause. "Oh no, tell her we're praying for her. Can she have visitors? Okay. No, David and I would like to come tomorrow, though. Even if we can't see her, we'd like to come pray with you. Okay. We'll be there tomorrow morning. Please keep me updated. Thank you for calling and letting me know. If there's anything else that David and I can do, please don't hesitate to ask." Macy hung up her phone and placed it on the kitchen counter, looking sad.

"Everything okay?" Claire asked.

Macy bit her bottom lip. "That was Reese's mom."

"Is Reese okay?"

"She's losing her second kidney. They're in the hospital now with her. It's a dire situation." Macy's eyes grew sad. "She's such a wonderful person. I've been praying so hard for her to find a kidney donor."

Claire clasped her hand to her lips. "Oh no. Do you know if she has found a match?"

Macy shook her head. "Not yet. I've been having coffee with her and bible study every week. You know, she's been doing dialysis, but we knew it couldn't last forever. She really needs a donor."

"I'm glad she has you. I really like her."

"Yeah, me too. She reminds me of you in a lot of ways," Macy spoke softly.

"Hey BayBay, when you going to get that pizza?" Jack yelled. "I'm starving."

Claire looked to Macy, and she smiled. "Go ahead. There's nothing we can do right now. She can't have visitors, anyway, but we're going to go to the hospital tomorrow."

Claire nodded. She walked into the living room and kissed Jack on the head. "Hey, you. I'm going to get the pizza now."

Jack nodded. "Love you," he called but never looked up. "Yes! A double play! Way to make a comeback after that error." He and David high-fived.

Claire smiled at her husband who loved baseball. She walked back to the kitchen where she saw Emmie covered in cheese puff residue. She laughed at her daughter and leaned in to kiss her on the forehead. "Emmie, mommy will be back in a few minutes. I'm going to get you and Gabe some pizza. Do you want pizza?"

Emmie nodded up and down. "Me ike piz. Momma no go. Momma no go."

Claire kissed her daughter again and hugged her tightly. "Mommy will be right back, sweetheart. Daddy's here, and Gabe's here to play with you."

CHAPTER TWENTY-SIX

As Claire pulled out of the garage, she turned on the radio. Her favorite song was playing, *Nothing Can Wash Away the Blood of Jesus*. She sang along as the music rang out. "What can wash away my sin? Nothing but the blood of Jesus. What can make me whole again? Nothing but the blood of Jesus."

As the song ended, Claire reflected on how much her life had changed over the past year. In just six months, Emmie would be two, and she felt sad that the time was passing so quickly. Her time with Emmie was amazing, and being a mother was everything she had hoped for.

She had seen an article on social media and learned that Emmie was Jack and Claire's rainbow baby. A rainbow baby was conceived after a miscarriage, and this thought comforted Claire. She had suffered so much after her miscarriage, and then during her pregnancy, the lingering fear of a miscarriage hung on. But in the end, Jesus gave her a beautiful rainbow baby that was a spitting image of herself and Jack. Emmie had green eyes like her father and had inherited her blond hair. Emmie's hair had ringlets that cascaded down her shoulders. She wore it high in ponytails because she complained it tickled her skin. Claire laughed, thinking of her daughter complaining.

Claire's stomach filled with butterflies when she thought of their decision to try for baby number two. Both she and Jack had siblings and wanted Charlotte to experience a world filled with siblings. She dreamed of three children but knew that they'd just have to rely on God's plan. *Can't tell God what to do,* she thought. *I learned that. It's all His way, in His time.* She and Jack had both agreed to not tell their family or David and Macy until they actually became pregnant. Keeping it between themselves would eliminate any additional pressure of answering questions constantly—especially from her mother.

Then her mind moved to her career. Claire's professional life had taken a new step during the past two years. She had recently received a promotion at work as a District Manager. This was an exciting move for her and her family, as this allowed her more flexibility in her career. She had seemingly adjusted nicely into her role and had established a travel routine that accommodated Jack's busy schedule. She had the flexibility to spend more time with Emmie and Jack, but Jack's workload was extremely heavy lately. He had been getting in late during the week since January. By the time he arrived home, she had usually put Emmie down for the evening. She and Emmie missed Jack for their family dinners, and often at bedtime, Emmie would face-time Jack. Claire was ready for Jack's caseload to lighten so he could get back in the routine of getting home at a decent time.

Then she smiled, thinking about her parents, who had recently made the decision to retire and move to Nashville from their hometown in Mississippi. They purchased a home less than seven miles from Jack and Claire's and anticipated making the move this summer. Her mother would begin babysitting Emmie on a full-time basis, which was comforting to Claire. She didn't enjoy leaving Emmie in a daycare, and she was thankful her mother had volunteered. Her father was going in a different direction after retirement; he decided to take a position as an online adjunct professor at one of the local community colleges. He seemed to be sad to not be practicing medicine any longer, but he seemed to be excited he was to have more time to spend with Emmie.

The twins were accepted to schools local to Nashville. Francis got into Hermitage University on a full academic scholarship. He had recently declared a major in Biology to attend medical school. Ezra was still undecided with his major and was enjoying his time playing baseball at Simon's College. And the last time she spoke to Ezra, he was holding true to not having a steady girlfriend. She laughed gently at her baby brothers. Completely different but identical twins.

Claire's mind shifted to her sister. Gabby was still living in downtown Nashville and working as a trauma nurse at the Regional hospital in Nashville. She finally had a steady boyfriend. Claire was excited about Gabby's beaux, Chad, since she had been the matchmaker. He was a rising attorney at Jack's firm, which meant Jack instantly liked him. They regularly had double dates, and the last date seemed to reveal that things were becoming serious. Jack even let it slip one night at bedtime that Chad had been shopping for rings. Claire was ecstatic for Gabby and could not wait for them to be married.

Claire's thoughts were interrupted, as she slowed to see that traffic was backed up. Suddenly, she made the decision to take the interstate to Antonio's, even though it was only ten miles away. They were doing construction on the two-lane road, and she didn't want to be stalled in the traffic. Besides, she was ready to return home and see Emmie. She maneuvered to the turning lane to exit toward the interstate.

As she entered the interstate, the lanes were congested with overflow traffic. She maneuvered to the far-left lane, and her phone rang. Claire looked to the phone stand and instantly realized she left it in her purse instead of placing it in the car holder. Traffic was heavy on the interstate, and she sped up to the maximum speed allotted. Her phone continued to ring, and with one hand, she unzipped her purse. She scrimmaged to find her phone and took a quick glance at her purse. Finally, she located her phone and turned her attention back to the road.

"What in the world?" Claire's brain couldn't comprehend what she was seeing. *Something isn't right.* Claire felt her face flush. *Is that truck heading toward me? It can't be.* Claire inhaled deeply as the red truck jumped over the guard rail and sped through the median. She pushed her horn and quickly looked to the right to see if she could merge. She couldn't. The car to her right was slowing down, but the car approaching was going too fast. Claire froze, and her foot slammed into the break.

"Jesus please, please help me. Dear God. No!" Claire yelled.

CHAPTER TWENTY-SEVEN

"JACK, I TRIED TO CALL CLAIRE TO REMIND her to get parmesan. She didn't answer," Macy called out from the kitchen.

"Okay, thanks. She probably got stuck in that construction they've been doing on Highway 71. It's awful. Supposedly, they'll be finished by the end of the month."

"A plum nightmare. It took me thirty minutes to get to church the other morning due to the congestion," David said as his phone flashed with a news alert. He clicked the article.

"What's up?" Jack asked nonchalantly.

"Bad wreck on the interstate, not too far from the entrance ramp. I hope Claire didn't get stuck in that traffic. It says traffic is backed up six miles because of the wreck." David placed his phone on the coffee table.

"Was anyone injured?" Macy asked.

"It just happened. Nothing's been posted yet."

"Goodness. I'm going to say a quick prayer for them." Macy closed her eyes, bowed her head, and prayed silently. When she was finished, she said, "David, I'm going to call the sitter and check on the girls. Can you and Jack keep an eye on Charlotte and Gabe please?"

"Sure thing. Tell them I love them." David grabbed Gabe's hand, and Jack took Emmie. "Come on kiddos; let's go play with the blocks." David slowly led them into the playroom.

As the kids played, Jack and David discussed the baseball season. The kids laughed as they built towers with their red and blue blocks. David noticed Macy standing by the door with her arms cross, and he knew her gesture usually meant trouble.

"What's wrong?" David asked. "The kids okay?"

"Yes, the kids are fine, and they send their love." She shook her head. "Have either of you heard from Claire yet? It's been over an hour since she left."

Jack looked down at his watch. "No, she hasn't called. I'll try her cell again." He pulled out his phone and dialed her number. The phone rang until her voicemail picked up. *It's Claire. Leave a message after the beep.* "That's strange, she typically answers. Especially since we have Emmie." He burrowed his eyes in concern. "That's twice we've called, and she hasn't answered."

"Maybe she forgot her phone," David said assuredly.

"No, I saw her take it," Macy corrected. "Jack, call Antonio's and see if she has picked up the pizza."

"Good idea. I'll do that now." Jack stood from the floor and patted Emmie on the head gently. "Be right back, Emmie."

Emmie smiled at him. Jack went into the kitchen and looked for the Antonio flyer with their phone number. He punched in the numbers and waited.

CHAPTER TWENTY-EIGHT

SHE COULDN'T BREATHE, AND SHE couldn't speak. Her eyes were plastered shut by something wet and thick. *Blood? Could that be blood holding my eyes closed?* Claire heard sirens and noises in the background—and voices shouting. *What are they saying?* Claire tried to take a deep breath, but it was impeded by something heavy. She couldn't inhale, and the small amount of air that filtered through her lungs sent trimmers down her spine. *What is on me?* Claire couldn't remember anything, and she couldn't move. *I'm stuck.*

"Miss, we're here to get you out. If you can hear us, give us a signal. A thumbs-up, blink your eyes, anything to let us know you hear us," the man called out.

Claire could hear his voice, but she still didn't understand who he was talking to. *Is he talking to me?* Claire tried to move her eyes and arms, but no movement happened. "I'm here. Hey, I'm here." She tried to speak. He didn't seem to hear her.

"Ma'am, you're going to hear a loud noise as we cut off your door. Don't be afraid." He leaned his hand into the crushed window and found her arm. He timed her pulse and waited to see if she responded to his touch.

"Tachycardia, no response to touch. We need to hurry and get her out," the man yelled.

Is he talking about me? She wanted to tell them she could hear them, but no words came out. *What happened*? *Why can't I remember what happened?*

A loud noise vibrated through her car, and it created a screeching metal sound. Claire could hear the sound, but it was faint, and strangely enough, it provided her a level of peace. Suddenly, she was so sleepy. She closed her eyes for one second, and then she snapped them open again. The next time, she closed her eyes for a little longer. *Ahhh, it feels so good. I just want to sleep.*

"I don't think she's going to make it. Is life flight here?" the man called out.

"Yeah, we're here. What's your initial assessment of her condition?" The flight nurse rushed up to Claire's car. "Any identification?"

"None found yet. The car's a mess. She hasn't responded to any stimuli. Initial assessment is heavy internal damage. The impact was head-on. Her heart rate is tachycardia, but her BP is all over the place. I don't know if she's gonna make it," he said grimly.

The nurse nodded. "Alright, let's get her out of there." The nurse crouched down to peer inside. "Hello, can you hear me?

Claire didn't respond.

"Found a purse," the police officer yelled. He pulled out a wallet and dusted off the glass. Her Id says her name is Claire St. John,"

"Claire? Claire? I'm nurse Nancy. Can you hear me, Claire?"

Claire's eyes snapped open when she recognized her name being called. *Me? They're talking about me?* "I can hear you! Help me! What's happening?"

"Claire be still and know that I'm here. The familiar male voice spoke. *"Claire, I have you in my arms. Don't be afraid."*

Jesus? Claire thought. *Is He here with me?*

Suddenly, a peace overcame her body, bringing a new understanding. Claire finally realized what was happening.

I'm dying. "Jesus, I'm scared," she said quietly. "My sweet Emmie and Jack. I don't want to leave them."

"Claire, don't fear death. There is no death—only eternal life." Then the male voice disappeared.

Claire felt her body lifting from the crunched metal, and instantly, excruciating pain radiated through her body. Claire felt the darkness enveloping her mind and body. She couldn't fight it, and she felt the world drift. Her blood pressure plummeted, and she crashed.

"Claire, stay with us. Fight, Claire," she heard the nurse say. "She's crashing. Start resuscitation."

"On my count, let's lift her onto the stretcher. One, Two, Three," another EMT said loudly.

"We have a pulse. It's threaded, but we have a pulse," Nurse Nancy yelled out.

Claire's mind awoke as her stretcher was placed on the helicopter, and she vaguely heard the rotor blades spinning, which created a movement of air. The machines within the helicopter beeped, and she felt needles sticking in her skin. As the helicopter rose into the sky, Claire felt the darkness take over again. She couldn't fight the urge to stay awake any longer, and as the helicopter flew toward the hospital, Claire closed her eyes again.

The life-flight chopper landed on the helipad, and flight nurses rushed Claire through the doors. "Caucasian Female. Name Claire St. John. Age 34. Tachycardia. BP/P is 68/48. HR is 152," Nurse Nancy called out. "On-site assessment is heavy damage to all areas of her body, possible head trauma, and she is unresponsive to verbal communication or stimuli. The patient has coded twice on the ride in."

"What type of accident are we talking about here?" the trauma surgeon asked.

"Head-on collision, sir. The patient's car is totaled, and the jaws of life was used to extract the patient from the vehicle."

"Let's get her to trauma room two. Stat, move it people!" he yelled.

CHAPTER TWENTY-NINE

JACK HUNG UP THE PHONE AND walked back to the playroom. He looked at David and Macy intensely. "Antonio's Pizza said Claire didn't pick up the pizza. Very strange. I called her cell phone again but still no answer."

"That *is* strange, Jack. Do you think something happened?" Macy asked nervously.

"I'm sure she's okay. Maybe a flat or stuck in that wreck traffic," David responded.

"I really don't know. She's never had a lack of communication." Jack checked his watch. "It's been about two hours since she left, correct?" Jack looked to Macy for confirmation.

Macy nodded.

The doorbell rang, and the trio looked at each other nervously.

"Were you expecting someone, Jack?" David asked.

Jack shook his head. "No." The doorbell rang again. "I'll get the door," Jack said. "Macy, can you watch Emmie and fix her a bite to eat please?"

"Sure. Come on, Emmie and Gabe. Let's get you kiddos fed."

"Me izza," Charlotte called out. "Me see momma."

"Shh, sweetie. Mommy will be home soon." Jack blew a kiss to his daughter and then turned to answer the door, but as he moved, a sense of dread crept up his spine.

He placed his hand on the doorknob and stalled in fear. The doorbell rang out for the third time, and with the sound, he shook his head and opened the door. Jack saw two police officers, and instantly, his mind went blank.

"Mr. St. John?" asked the first officer.

"Yes." Jack looked from one to the other. "I'm Jack St. John."

"Related to Claire St. John?" the second officer asked.

"Yes, Claire is my wife." Jack looked confused.

The police officers took their hats off. "Mr. St. John, may we come in for a moment? It's concerning your wife, Claire."

Jack mindlessly backed away from the door to allow them entrance. In slow motion, he pointed toward the living room. They followed behind him, but Jack looked back, watching their movements, and instantly, he knew that his BayBay wasn't coming home.

"Would you like to sit?" Jack asked politely.

"No sir, we'll stand. Mr. St. John, I'm officer Phillips. This is my partner, Officer McKenzie."

"Officers, not to be short, but could you please tell me why you're here about Claire?" Jack eyed them as tears crowded his eyes.

The officer nodded. "Yes, sir." He stopped as Macy and David entered the living room.

Macy drew in an audible breath at the sight of the officers. She grabbed David's hands as tears filled her eyes.

"This is our best friends. You can speak freely in front of them," Jack confirmed.

"Yes sir," the second officer spoke.

"Mr. St. John, there was an accident a little while ago on I43. Mrs. St. John was involved in the accident." The first officer paused and surveyed the group.

"Claire, was in the accident? Please continue." Jack held his hand over his mouth.

"A vehicle traveling west bound collided with a vehicle traveling east bound, which was registered to Mrs. St. Johns. The two vehicles collided head-on."

"What!" Macy yelled.

Jack ignored Macy and stared at the policeman. "Officer, my wife? Is she okay?"

Macy fell to her knees and let out a wail. David put his hand on her shoulder. Jack kept his eyes on the officer.

Jack spoke very softly. "Is Claire okay?"

"We were notified that Mrs. St. John is alive and being airlifted to Southeast Regional Trauma Center in critical condition."

"Alive? Oh, thank God; she's alive," Jack said as emotion overcame him. "Can I see her?"

"You'll need to go to the Southeast Regional Trauma Center. We'll be more than happy to escort you, sir."

"Yes, please." Jack inhaled deeply to find courage. "All that matters is that she's alive. Whatever's wrong, we can face that." Jack looked at Macy and David. "Can you please call Beth and Mica? And My parents and Nolan? And Gabby. Oh God, what's happening?" Jack inhaled again and bent over to put his hands on his knees. His knees shook under his hands. He quietly prayed, "Jesus, give me strength in this moment."

David came from behind and gently laid his hand on Jack's shoulder. "Jack, just breathe. Macy and I will take care of everything you need. You go to Claire."

"Um . . . Emmie . . ." He regained his stature with panic etched into his face.

"We got her. Go, Jack. Go." Macy cried as she spoke.

Jack hurried to grab Emmie. "Emmie, daddy has to go see mommy. Okay? You be good now." He touched his finger to her nose. "I love you to the moon and back."

"Momma, me iss momma." Charlotte hugged Jack.

"Yes, you'll get to kiss momma soon." Jack choked back the panic to keep from frightening his daughter. Jack picked up his keys and headed to the garage. He looked back at Macy, David, Emmie, and Gabe.

"Keep us updated on her condition," David called.

Jack nodded as he walked to the mudroom door. "She's going to be okay," he said aloud to convince himself.

After three attempts, Jack finally was able to unlock the car door. His hands still shaking, he slid into the leather seat, and his eye focused on their family beach photo on the dashboard.

"Oh BayBay, look at us."

Jack pulled his head up and backed out of the garage. He saw the police cruiser situated at the lead of his neighborhood road. He pulled behind the officers, and they took the lead. As he drove toward the hospital, his mind replayed the events of the day.

"She only went to get a pizza. A stupid pizza." Jack hit his steering wheel with the palm of his hand. "Did I even tell her I love her? Oh, Jesus, please help us. I'm so scared I'll never see her again." Jack let the tears flow.

As the entrance to the interstate approached, Jack hyperventilated. He drew in quick, deep breaths to control his breathing. His heart cracked as he saw the remains of Claire's car on the back of a tow truck.

"Oh Claire, my sweet Claire. Why you? Why us?" Jack screamed.

The officer's words played over in his mind. *Life flighted. Critical.* Jack knew deep in his gut that the officers were trying to prepare him for the worst.

Jack prayed as they continued down the interstate toward the hospital. "Jesus, I don't know what's happening right now. The love of my life is fighting for her life. Jesus, I lift her up and ask that you heal any injuries. Dear God, please hear me."

The ringing of his phone interrupted his prayer. *It's Beth.* He hesitated to answer the call.

"Jesus help me to stay strong." He pressed the button to answer the call. "Beth?" Jack asked.

"Oh Jack, how is my baby?" Beth asked hysterically.

"Beth, I'm not at the hospital, yet. I don't know."

"Dear God. David called and told Mica she was life-flighted."

"Yeah, that's as much as I know now. The officers said she was critical." Jack couldn't contain his emotions, and a sob escaped his lips.

"Oh, sweetheart, we're on our way. We're headed to the airport to take the next flight to Nashville. Oh, I can't believe this happening. My sweet Claire. Why Claire?" Beth dropped the phone.

"Jack, how are you holding up?" Mica asked.

"Not sure right now, Mica."

"Jack, stay strong. Claire needs you to be strong when you get there."

"Yes, sir."

"Son, when you see her, make sure she knows how much we love her." Mica paused. "Jack, she's going to be okay. I just know she will."

"Yes, sir."

"Goodbye, son. We'll see you at the hospital shortly." Mica hung up the phone.

Jack turned quickly into the trauma center's main parking area. He found a spot close to the entrance and swerved in. Jack's hands were still shaking as he pulled the handle of the car door. He took in a deep breath, pushed the door open, and placed his feet flat on the ground. As he stood, his legs shook, and he fell against the door and dropped his head into his hands.

"Mr. St. John?"

Jack looked up at one of the police officers who had escorted him. "Yes?"

"Sir, are you okay?"

"I think so," Jack responded.

"Mr. St. John, you'll need to go into the emergency room. Once inside, go to the admission desk, and they'll be able to direct you from there."

Jack nodded. "Thank you for your help, officers."

"Yes, sir." The officers tipped their hats and headed to their patrol car.

Jack looked both ways and crossed to the hospital doors. As the emergency room doors opened, he couldn't remember where the officers told him to go. He panicked slightly as sounds of clamor filled the emergency room.

Jack scanned his surroundings, suppressing his panic. Out of the corner of his eye, he spotted an older lady with salty-grey hair. She sat at a desk and held her hand up gently to signal his attention. Jack responded with a nod and slowly walked toward her.

"Hi, what can I help you with?" she asked.

"My wife was brought here. By life flight," Jack stuttered.

"Sir, what is your wife's name? Also, can you provide your driver's license so I may verify your information?"

"Claire. Um. Claire St. John." Jack handed her his driver's license.

She keyed information into the hospital computer system and looked up to Jack. "Mrs. St. John was brought in a little bit of ago. She's in surgery now. Follow this hall and go to the fifth floor. Once you step off the elevator, you'll see another reception desk. That's the Critical Care Unit. They'll be able to provide you more information regarding your wife."

"Thank you." Jack slowly started toward the elevator.

CHAPTER THIRTY

"WHERE IS THAT CT SCAN I ORDERED?" the trauma surgeon yelled.

"It's coming in now, doctor," the nurse replied as she inserted an IV into Claire's arm.

"Get neurology in here!" he yelled.

"IV is in. Her BP is falling again, Doctor."

"What is it?

"Neuro is here," someone called out.

"BP is 63/45. Heart rate is 145."

"Okay, guys and gals! Let's save a life today!"

"Doc, CT results are up," the nurse said.

The trauma surgeon reviewed the results and held his hand up to his cheek. *Not good*, he thought. "Swelling in her abdomen, looks like the liver is lacerated." He turned to her abdomen and tested for rigidity. "Rigid and not pliable to touch. Get that intubation going, now. Let's move it, people. We need to get her to surgery. NOW!" he yelled out.

Claire faded in and out of consciousness, and her body felt so cold. She heard close, rushed voices. Her mind didn't feel right, and Claire still only saw darkness. She tried to open her eyes but was unsuccessful. She couldn't move her fingers, and when she tried speaking, nothing came out of her mouth. *Help me. Help me,* she thought over and over. Pain radiated through her throat as something slid into her mouth. *A tube. What's happening?* The intubation tube slid down her trachea, and she panicked as she felt the movement crowding her airway. Her body shook on the hospital bed, and she felt hands push down on her body. *Jesus, help me. I'm so scared.* Then, she faded back into the darkness.

"Seizure! She is seizing," the nurse yelled.

"Push 4 mg of Lorazepam, now," the trauma surge called.

"Pushing."

The room waited to see her response.

"Seizure is clear," he called out. "Move it, people; we need to prep her for surgery ASAP," the trauma surgeon yelled.

"Neuro is here," yelled another nurse.

"Immense swelling on the brain with significant brain bleeding; we need to move, people."

The room scrambled, and as they wheeled her out into the hall, a nurse yelled out, "She's coding again! Code Blue!"

"Someone grabbed the crash cart, stat."

The trauma surgeon began chest compressions. "Come on, Claire. Fight. We need you to fight."

"We have a pulse; it's weak, but it's a pulse."

CHAPTER THIRTY-ONE

JACK WRUNG HIS HANDS IN FRUSTRATION. No one had given him an update on Claire beyond telling him that she was in surgery. The nurse only told him that the surgery could last upward to ten hours, depending on Claire's needs. He checked his watch and gasped, realizing he had not seen Claire's face in four hours.

"BayBay, I'm here. You're not alone. I love you so much," he murmured.

Jack's mind raced back to the moment they married. He stood at the alter scared of what marriage would hold for them. He was young, just finished college, and had freshly passed the bar exam. His hopes were to provide a wonderful home for her, but he doubted himself. Jack's fears completely vanished when she appeared between the wooden double doors of the church. There she stood, the most beautiful woman in the world. Her white gown was long with a veil that transcended four feet past the hem of her gown. She wore her blonde hair long down her back, and her lips were painted pink. She held pink roses in one hand, and as she stepped into the Church, she lifted the front of her dress with the other hand to show Jack her pink Converse tennis shoes. They both laughed, and he knew at that moment, she would always be her BayBay.

Jack's memories were interrupted by his phone vibrating in his pocket. "Hello?"

"Jack, honey, it's Mom."

"Hi, Mom," Jack responded numbly. "Did Macy call you?"

"Yes, love. Oh, Jack, honey, I don't know what to say. We love you and Claire. We're praying for her."

"Thanks, Mom." He paused. "Are you coming?"

"We're catching the next flight out. We probably won't make it to Nashville until ten o'clock tonight."

"Okay, mom."

"Do you have any updates?"

"No, nothing."

"Jack, I love you. Dad loves you."

"I love y'all. Mom, I have to go. I'm sorry, but I just can't talk right now."

"Okay, honey. We're praying, and we'll be there as soon as our plane lands." She hung up the phone.

He continued to lean against the window and stared out over the bustling city. Below, the city shined brightly with lights and signs, people on the streets continuing with their daily routine. Cars sped up and down the streets, children ate ice cream, and tourists mulled around, enjoying the scenery. He turned and looked at the pale, white walls of the waiting room. A coffee machine was situated in the corner with a makeshift kitchen. A few families were spread out throughout the room, but Jack still spoke aloud, not caring if they thought he was crazy for talking to himself. "Jesus, what have we done to fail you? We've tried to be obedient. Why, Jesus? Why Claire? What about our family?"

Before he saw them, he heard his name called. "Jack?"

He turned toward the entrance and saw Beth with Mica by her side. Beth's face was red and splotchy. Her hair was messy, and she held a Kleenex in her right hand. Mica, strong and calm, looked as though he had been run over by a freight train. His eyes were puffy and red, and his face was drawn tightly, which made him look much older. Jack held up his hand in acknowledgment.

"Oh, Jack." Beth went forward and held her arms out to embrace Jack.

"Beth, Mica." Jack leaned into Beth's embrace and let her squeeze him tightly.

"Any updates about my baby?"

Jack stepped back and motioned toward the seats near the window. "Let's sit."

Mica led the way and sat. "What did the doctor say?"

"I haven't seen a doctor yet."

"What?"

"Mica, why wouldn't a doctor come? Beth asked, confused.

"Jack, who's providing the updates? Is she in surgery?"

"Yeah. She's in surgery. One of the intensive care nurses is providing updates. She promised to come in and update as often as possible. Claire's been in surgery for about an hour now, I guess. I'm sorry I'm not very helpful."

"Of course not, son. It's a lot to take in. I'll see if I can get someone to update me." Mica left the waiting room.

Beth patted Jack's hand and blew her nose with the other hand. "I just don't understand all this. My baby. I just don't understand."

"Me either. She was just going to get us a pizza. How does something like this happen to us?"

"Oh, Jack, bad things happen to good people all the time. What about my grandshug? Is she okay?"

"Macy and David are watching her. What will I tell Emmie?" he asked sadly.

"Nothing yet, Jack. Claire's a fighter. I've never seen my sweet Claire lose a battle."

Jack looked up as the twins and Gabby entered the room.

"Hey," the twins said with their heads hanging.

"Any word?" Francis asked.

"Not yet, buddy," Jack responded.

"Oh, Momma." Gabby ran over to Beth and laid her head in Beth's lap.

"Shhhhh, now, sweet one. It's all going to be okay. Your sister is a strong one. We know she won't stop fighting. She loves little Emmie way too much to not fight."

"Mica?" Jack asked as he reentered the room.

"It's not good. I spoke with the nurse, and she updated me slightly. Claire's brain has swelled, and she sustained internal bleeding."

"What's that mean?" Ezra asked.

"Son, your sister is injured *inside* her body, which means they need to operate to fix her up. She has a lacerated liver, swelling of the brain. We need to be prepared for the worst," Mica said gravely.

"NO! Not my Claire," Beth screamed.

Jack couldn't comprehend what Mica's words meant. He suddenly felt woozy. He stood up and walked to the coffee machine. He stared at the choices and fought back the tears as he picked up two cups—one for Claire and one for himself. He poured the coffee and made her a cup with cream and sugar. He took a sip and held his head back as sorrow consumed him. His phone was ringing, and he silenced it. He knew he couldn't deal with anyone else. Jack walked back to the chairs with his two coffee cups.

"Did you bring me a cup, too, sugar?" Beth asked.

"No. One for me, and one for Claire," Jack said.

"But honey, Claire . . ."

"One for me, and one for Claire," Jack said louder, and then he closed his eyes and shook his head. When he opened his eyes, he drank Claire's coffee, and then he drank his.

"Jack, have you eaten anything?" Mica looked at his son-in-law with concern.

"Not since earlier today. Claire was bringing dinner home. Pizza," he said numbly.

"Boys, go to the cafeteria and grab Jack something to eat." Mica handed the boys some money. "Anyone else care for something? We may be waiting a while."

CHAPTER THIRTY-TWO

THE HOURS TICKED BY, AND THE intensive care nurse visited frequently. As the clock approached eleven p.m., a doctor in scrubs entered the waiting room. He looked tired, and his face was emotionless. Jack saw him enter and gently elbowed Mica to gain his attention.

"St. John family?" the doctor called out.

Jack raised his hand and stood. "I'm Jack St. John."

The doctor walked toward Jack and extended his hand. "Hello, Sir. Are you Claire St. John's next of kin?"

"Yes, I'm her husband." He turned to point toward the Klines. "This is her mother and father and siblings."

"Hello. I'm Martin Vandergross. I'm the chief trauma surgeon here."

"Hello, Dr. Vandergross. I'm Dr. Ezra Kline, Claire's father, and this is her mother, Beth."

"Sir, Ma'am." He nodded. "Why don't you follow me to the family private room where we can have privacy? Then, I can update you on Claire's condition." He motioned for them to follow.

They slowly walked down the white hospital hallway and entered the family room. "Is she alive?" Jack blurted out.

"I'm sorry. I don't know why that just came out of my mouth."

"Yes. Claire is alive," Doctor Vandergross responded. "Please sit."

"Oh, thank Jesus." Beth placed her hand over her heart.

"I'm going to be very straight with you regarding Claire's condition." He surveyed their seated posture. "Claire has experienced an extreme amount of injury to her body. She isn't currently breathing on her own; we had to intubate her. She has coded four times since the accident, and she had a seizure. We're treating her as best we can. Claire's brain has suffered damage, and neurology has removed a portion of her skull to prevent the swelling from being restricted."

"How much damage to her brain?" Jack asked.

"At this time, it's hard to know, exactly. She hasn't responded to any stimuli. She hasn't moved when asked or hasn't verbally communicated since the wreck."

"No! Jesus No! My baby girl." Beth gasped, and Gabby squeezed her mother.

"Do you think she's brain dead?" Micah asked solemnly.

"Well, we haven't even gotten that far yet, Dr. Kline. We have to deal with the brain swelling first. We'll test brain activity later, if she makes it through the night."

Beth wailed.

"You've seen a lot of these cases, Doc," Ezra said. "What's your opinion? Do you think she'll make it?"

Dr. Vandergross sighed. "Professionally, I can't say one way or another, but I want to be honest with you, Dr. Kline. I would be surprised if she survived the night. I'm sorry."

"Oh Jesus," Jack said.

Dr. Vandergross waited. "I know this information is a lot to take in. Claire is in the critical care unit, and we'll allow her to have two visitors at a time."

"Can I go now?" Jack asked.

"Mr. St. John, absolutely, but I want to caution you on her state. When you see her, she may not resemble herself."

Jack shook his head in acknowledgment.

"I'll keep you updated on her condition throughout the night. The next twelve hours are critical. If Claire does make it through the night, we'll start to assess her brain functionality." He stood and extended his hand to Mica. "Dr. Kline."

"Dr. Vandergross."

"Jack, when you're ready to see her, let the nurse at the station know." Dr. Vandergross nodded and exited the waiting room.

Jack inhaled a deep breath, and shivers crept up his arms. "I don't care what he says. She's going to make it. We all know she's strong."

"Of course, Jack. My baby girl is a fighter. She'll be just fine. You wait and see." Beth dropped her head into her hands and cried.

"Jack, do you want to see her alone?" Mica asked.

"Yes, please. I need to be with her. I need to hold her hand." Tears ran down his cheek. "I don't know what God's plan is, but I know I can't live without her."

"Jack, honey."

Jack turned to see his parents and his brother. "Oh mom, you're here." He fell into his mother's arms.

"Of course, my love. I'm always here." She stroked his hair.

Charles embraced his wife and son. Jack smelled his mother's perfume, and normalcy filled his senses. "It can't be real, mom. She was just going to get us a pizza. I don't even think I told her I love her before she left. I was watching a stupid ballgame, and I didn't even pay her any attention. Oh, mom."

"Shhh honey. She knows how much you love her. Jack, she loves you and Emmie more than anything. She's going to fight to stay with you."

Jack nodded and wiped his eyes. "Okay, I'm going to see her. Can someone call and check on Emmie, please?"

"I'll do it." Gabby pulled her phone out and dialed Macy's number.

CHAPTER THIRTY-THREE

WHEN JACK SAW CLAIRE, HE LOST HIS footing. He grasped the glass sliding door to steady himself. Bile rose in his throat, but he swallowed it down. "No," he whispered. "Oh, Jesus, please, no."

His feet were heavy as he tried to lift them. Jack froze at the entrance of the room, and his mind raced with the images. Claire's room was full of machines attached to her body. She lay lifeless on the bed, and the room purred from the sound produced by the machines. Her chest rose and fell with the pump of each mechanical breath. Her blonde hair was stained with blood. Her face was swollen, bruised, and disfigured. She didn't look like his Claire.

He slowly walked to the side of the bed. The smell of blood and flesh filled his nostrils. He picked up her hand and gently cupped it into his. "BayBay, can you hear me? I'm here, Claire. I will always be here." He sniffled back the tears. "Emmie is waiting for you. BayBay, if you can hear me, squeeze my hand. Come on, Claire. Let me know you're still here."

Claire didn't respond.

"Excuse me, Mr. St. John. Do you need anything?"

The nurse went to Claire's catheter and checked the urine output.

"Sorry, I didn't hear you come in." He looked at the IV bag.

"I didn't mean to startle you. I just needed to check Mrs. St. John's urine output."

He nodded. "Can I ask you something?"

"Yes," she responded softly.

"Do you think she can hear me?" Jack asked.

"Absolutely. I believe she can hear all of us. She's strong, and she's fighting. Otherwise, we would've lost her hours ago."

"Thank you, Nurse . . . ?"

"Abigail. Just call me Abby. I'll be right outside the door if you need me." Abby pulled the glass door shut.

Jack laid his head gently on the side of Claire's bed without removing his hand from hers. "I'm so sorry. I should've been the one to go get the pizza. Oh, Claire. I love you so much. Please honey, please forgive me. It should be me, not you," he whispered.

Jack laid with his head down until the nurse made her rounds again.

He looked up as she entered the room. "What time is it?" he asked hoarsely.

"It's a little after midnight," she responded as she began to change out Claire's IV bag. "Mr. St. John, visiting hours will end soon."

Jack nodded.

"Stay a little while longer. I'll let you know when the visiting hours have ended."

"Okay, thank you." Jack stood to stretch his legs. He

went to the window and looked out. "Claire, do you remember the time we took Emmie to the zoo?" He looked back to Claire. "Remember how she loved the tigers so much that she begged us to buy the stuffed one? I didn't want to because I was afraid we were spoiling her, but you, oh you, my love, couldn't say no. What was it she named that tiger? Oh, man I can't remember." Jack walked back toward Claire and gently grabbed her hand. "Do you remember, Claire? If you do, squeeze my hand." He paused. "Claire let me know you hear me. Please, honey. Please."

Suddenly, Jack bounded from his chair and ran to the nurse's station.

"She squeezed! Abby, she squeezed my hand," he said.

"Mr. St. John, I'll be right there," Abby said, and Jack bolted back into the room.

"Claire, do it again. Squeeze my hand. Come on, BayBay."

"Mr. St. John, Abby tells me you felt a squeeze," a voice said.

Jack was surprised to see Dr. Vandergross standing in front of nurse Abby.

"Yes sir. I was telling her a story about our daughter, and she squeezed."

Dr. Vandergross checked the electroencephalogram and recorded the activity on her chart. He took his light and opened Claire's eyes, one by one. He then placed his ink pen on her cheek and pressed gently. He moved to her hand and pinched slightly. "Abby, no reflex present." He went to Claire's feet and uncovered them from the white sheet. He ran the pen up from her heel to her toes. "Again, no reflex present." He covered Claire's feet and placed his pen back into his coat pocket. "Jack. May I call you that?"

"Yes sir."

"Jack, unfortunately, Claire is showing no signs of brain activity yet. Sometimes patients will have involuntary reflex motions. This could be caused by the body's distress, a posturing reflex, or possibly a seizure onset. Either way Jack, Claire has yet to show a sign."

"It felt so real."

"Jack, it *is* real, but the involuntary response does not necessarily mean that she heard you and is responding to you. In all honesty, we don't know if she can hear you, but it definitely doesn't hurt to talk to her, just in case. And I'm here to monitor *any* change in status, so let Abby know if you need anything, okay? I'll leave you and Claire alone for a while. Abby, we're going to let Mr. St. John stay beyond the regular visiting hours, if he wants."

Abby nodded.

"Thank you." Jack went back to his seat and placed his hand on Claire's cheek. "I love you. I don't want to lose you. Please, oh please, stay with me." Jack laid his head on Claire's bed and fell asleep.

CHAPTER THIRTY-FOUR

"DADDA!" EMMIE RAN AND JUMPED into her father's arms. "Me miss you dadda! Me see mommy?"

"Hey, sweet girl. Daddy missed you." Jack nestled his head into Emmie's hair. "Hey guys, thanks for bringing her."

"Of course." Macy placed the backpack down. "How is she?"

"Mom, can you and dad take Emmie down to the cafeteria for a snack?"

"Well, of course. Come on, honey. Let's go get you some juice," Donna replied.

"Me luv juice. Me luv grape. Me see momma?" Emmie walked happily toward the cafeteria with Donna and Charles.

"Jack, how are you holding up?" David asked.

"As good as can be expected."

"How is she?" Macy asked again.

"Well, she made it through the night. She coded around five am, but they were able to . . . to revive her. We're supposed to get an update around seven-thirty."

"That's good news, right? She survived the night. Didn't they say if she made it through, she might be okay?"

"Not really. They haven't done the tests yet, but they don't think her brain is active. She twitched yesterday, but they didn't think it was anything more than an involuntary reflex."

Macy gasped.

"The doctor thinks she is completely brain dead. They're supposed to do an EEG at some point today to confirm there's no brain activity." Jack closed his eyes. "I don't even want to hear the results. That would be the end of my hope."

"Oh, Jack. I don't know what to say," David said.

"No one seems to know, David."

"I can't believe this happening. Oh, Jack, I can't imagine what you're going through. I love her like a sister; she is my dearest friend," Macy said.

"I know. And she loves you. The only thing anyone can do is pray. Pray she wakes up. Pray she makes it. Pray we stay strong."

"Absolutely Jack. We've prayed since the moment the officers arrived. Would you like some coffee? I can grab it for us."

"Thanks, Macy. I'll take two cups. One with cream and sugar and one black, please."

"Two?"

"I drink Claire's for her—and mine."

"Of course. Have you slept any? You look so tired."

"I fell asleep with Claire for a bit." He paused. "I can't lose her." Jack tried to hold back the tears but failed.

David walked and put his hand on Jack's shoulder, "Jack, Jesus is in control. We will be faithful in our prayers and ask that He heal her completely. Psalm 46 verse 1 says,

'God is our refuge and strength, a very present help in trouble.' He is in control, Jack, and Claire's fate relies on him."

"Thank you, David. We need all the prayers we can get. I need a moment, please." Jack walked to the restroom and closed the door.

"David." Mica extended his hand.

"Good to see you again, Mica."

"I wish it was better circumstances." Mica looked toward the lobby windows.

"Me as well. Is there anything I can do to assist y'all?"

"I wish. But unfortunately, it's a waiting game at this point. It's tough to watch your child suffer. As a parent, you never imagine losing a child before yourself. As a doctor, I've lost patients over the years, but never a patient's child. You don't seem to ever be prepared for something like this."

"I cannot imagine the pain you and your family are enduring. I'm so sorry, Mica, and I wish Macy and I could do something to make it better."

"That's kind of you to say." His attention turned to the nurse entering the waiting room.

"Mr. St. John?" the nurse called out.

Jack opened the bathroom door, wiping tears from his eyes. "I'm here."

"Good morning. I hope you were able to get some rest."

"Not really. But thanks," he said quickly.

"Could you follow me to your wife's room, please? The doctor would like to speak to you."

"Is everything okay?" he asked nervously.

"Just please follow me; the doctor will provide you with the details."

"Okay." He turned his attention to his family and friends. "Beth and Mica, do you want to go in?

Beth nodded. She grabbed Mica's hand and looked toward Macy and David. "If y'all can just hang out here, we'll update you as soon as we return."

As they followed the nurse down the hall, Jack could see various family members visiting with their loved ones. He walked slowly as they approached Claire's room. As he entered, two doctors seemed to be assessing Claire.

"Good morning, Jack."

"Hi, Dr. Vandergross." He extended his hand out.

"Good morning Dr. and Mrs. Kline."

"Good morning," Mica responded.

"I want to introduce you to Dr. Hill. Dr. Hill is the neurologist that has been treating Claire." Dr. Vandergross pointed to his clipboard. "Dr. Hill has finished her assessment of Claire's neurological stance, and I have completed my assessment of Claire's status as well."

Dr. Hill nodded to the family. "Mr. St. John, I wish I had better news to deliver. After reviewing Claire's EEG and her other neurological tests, we believe Claire is essentially brain dead."

"No! No!" Beth's scream pierced the room. Mica wrapped Beth into his arms.

"What does *essentially* mean?" Jack asked numbly.

"I know this hard to hear, but we need you to understand what's happening to her body."

"Dr. Vandergross, she made it through the night. She survived," Jack murmured. "You didn't think she would."

He nodded his head. "Yes, she did, Jack, but unfortunately, Claire's body is shutting down, and her organs are starting to fail."

Jack stared at Dr. Hill motionless. He felt his mouth open, but no sound erupted.

Dr. Hill continued, "Mr. St. John, we don't believe Claire is with us anymore."

"I don't understand," Jack spoke softly.

"This is never easy to say. I wish I could give you more hope, but your wife is dying. She has no brain activity, and even though her heart may be pumping, the rest of her organs *will* quit working with no brain activity. It's just a matter of time."

"No, you don't understand. I . . . I can't lose her. I . . . just . . ." Jack stammered trying to catch his breath.

Doctor Vandergross interjected, "Jack, take a deep breath. Breathe for me."

Jack inhaled deeply and felt his head get woozy.

Mica held Jack's arm in support. "Son, there's a decision that needs to be made. And Claire needs you to be strong."

Jack looked into Mica's eyes and nodded. "What are my choices?"

Dr. Hill answered, "You can keep Claire on the ventilator to prolong her death, or we can take her off the life support."

Jack stood silent. Finally, he said, "Prolong her death?"

"Yes. As I said earlier, we can keep her breathing, but eventually, all of her organs will fail. Sometimes that takes a week. Sometimes a year."

Jack sucked in a breath.

"There's also a third option. Claire is an organ donor."

"Oh, God! Help me!" Jack fell to the floor.

Through the glass, some of the nurses saw Jack fall, and they ran into the room. "He's fine. Back away from him." Dr. Vandergross kneeled next to him. "Jack, if there was any hope, any response, or any stimuli, we could keep fighting. Her brain isn't working; her organs are dying."

Jack exhaled. He took his hand and wiped his eyes. "How do you let go of the one person you love most in this world? How do you do that?"

"I can't answer that for you, Jack. I just know that she's not here anymore."

"Oh, God. No," Beth wailed.

"Jack, would it be okay if I bring in your parents?" Doctor Vandergross asked, motioning to the nurse on duty.

"Yes. I can't make this decision alone." "Oh, God. What do I do?" He turned to Beth and Mica. "Beth, Micah, what do I do?" he asked. "I can't let her go. I just can't." He was barely audible.

Beth wailed again. Tears filled Micah's eyes. "I . . . uh . . . I . . ." Sobs erupted from his lips, and he couldn't finish his sentence.

"Spend some time with Claire," Doctor Vandergross said. "Spend time talking with your family."

"How much time do I have to decide?"

Doctor Vandergross looked around the room. "Not as much as you want. If you decide to donate her organs, we need to preserve them for transplant pretty quickly, before they fail."

Jack stood up and looked at Claire—his sweet, sweet Claire. How could she not be here? Jack walked to Claire's bed and placed his hand on her swollen cheek. "BayBay, they told me you're not here. I don't believe them. Please wake up. Please stay with me. You can't leave me. You promised to be with me forever."

"Jack, I love you." Claire spoke from the corner of the room. She was dressed in a white gown, and she held their baby boy in her arms. Claire looked at her husband, and her heart ached for his suffering. If only he could see her now, with their beautiful son, he would understand the peace and joy she felt.

"Jack, honey," Donna said as she and Charles entered Claire's room. Nolan, Gabby, Ezra, and Francis followed them.

"Mom, it's bad," he said numbly. "Where's Emmie?"

"She's with Macy and David," Donna replied softly.

Jack nodded and turned his attention back to Claire.

Beth leaned over closely, "Claire, shugs. Momma is here," she said as she rubbed Claire's hand.

"Momma, oh momma. Don't be sad. I'm happy and at peace. You have a grandson that will be waiting with me for the day we are reunited," Claire spoke gently. She knew they couldn't hear her.

"Now, Claire, it's time to wake up and show these fools they don't know what they're talking about. Now you've had enough of that beauty sleep. You hear me, Claire? Wake up," Beth spoke sternly.

"Claire, love, it's Daddy. Fight, baby girl. Fight for us. Emmie is in the waiting room. She misses you, Claire."

"Oh daddy, I love you and will forever be waiting for you. Kiss my Emmie and let her know her brother and I will watch over her always."

Jack sniffled and wiped his nose. "The doctors think we should let her go. They said she's not here."

"Hogwash. My baby girl is here," Beth said.

"Claire is an organ donor," Gabby spoke out.

Jack turned to see Gabby hiding in the corner. "Gabby, you can come closer." Gabby shook her head and backed further away.

"Don't be afraid, Gabby. You're right. Fight for my organs to help other people. You are so brave. I love you, sis." Claire reached out and touched Gabby's shoulder.

Gabby flinched as she felt a light touch.

"Gabby, are you okay?" Francis asked.

Gabby nodded and went closer to the bed where Claire's body lay. "She would give the gift of life to someone else if she could," Gabby said softly.

"Gabby, don't say that! That's your sister," Beth said sharply. "Do you want them cutting her up and passing out her organs?"

"Mom, I don't want to lose her, either. But if she not going to live, we have to honor her wish to donate her organs.

"I agree with Gabby," Micah said.

"Oh, how could you Mica? That's our baby."

"Beth, you heard the doctors. Our child is gone. She's brain dead. Her organs are going to die. We can give them to someone else so she can live on."

Jack held up his hand. "Stop it. Just be quiet. I can't deal with this." Jack leaned over and kissed Claire's cheek. "I love you so much. And this hurts so much. Claire, what do I do? I need you."

"Jack, my love." Claire gracefully glided to Jack's side. *"I'm not there anymore, my love."* Claire leaned into

Jack's ear. *"Let me go, my love. I'm ready to go. Your son and I will be waiting for you."*

Jack raised his hand to his ear and opened his mouth. "Claire?" he whispered.

Suddenly, the machines began to beep. Jack looked from Claire to the monitors.

The trauma team rushed forward, led by Doctor. Vandergross.

"She's flatlining," a nurse called out.

Dr. Vandergross looked at Jack. "We have to resuscitate if you want to donate her organs. I need a decision now."

"It's time, Claire," the male voice spoke.

Claire nodded with a smile and turned to face Jack. She whispered gently into his ear, *"Jack, I will always love you. I'll be waiting for you, and we will be reunited."* Claire's spirit disappeared from the room.

Jack felt Claire fill him with peace, and he shook his head. "Resuscitate her. She wants her organs donated." He closed his eyes and spoke aloud, "Claire, I will love you forever."

CHAPTER THIRTY-FIVE

JACK AND EMMIE HELD HANDS AS they walked behind Claire's casket. Jack had let Gabby and Beth pick Claire's casket.

"Oh Claire, if you could only see the casket your family has picked for you," he whispered. They had chosen a light pink casket for Claire, one trimmed with white lining, and Emmie had added her favorite fuzzy bear to the inside. He squeezed Emmie's hand and entered the church.

As he stood at the entrance, he glanced around the seating area and was not surprised by the volume of individuals in attendance. Claire was loved by so many, and their presence proved this. He bent down to pick Emmie up, and he saw Reese on the last row, sitting in a wheelchair. He waived gently.

She returned his wave and mouthed, "Thank you."

Jack nodded with tears in his eyes. He walked slowly to the front row, and once there, he lowered Emmie onto the pew and sat down. "Oh BayBay, if you could see all these people." He closed his eyes. "Oh, my Claire, how I miss you." He saw an image of Claire's face, and his heart thumped as the sound of *Amazing Grace* filled the Church.

Beth reached for Jack's hand and squeezed it tightly. "Jack, are you okay?"

"I don't know if I'll ever be okay," he whispered. "I miss her so much."

"Me too. Me too." She shook her head.

"As we come today to celebrate the life of Claire St. John, Jack would like to speak. Jack?" David motioned toward Jack.

"David, thank you." Jack made his way to the front of her casket. He pulled out a piece of paper. "I'm sorry if this isn't as professional as it could be." The crowd murmured sympathies. He looked up from his paper and saw sadness. He shook his head. "As you may know, Claire and I met in college. She has been the one and only love of my life since the day I saw her. It was love at first sight for me—and many sights later for her."

A small rumble of laughter erupted.

"You see, Claire would not want us to be sad. She would want us to rejoice that she is in Heaven." He surveyed the room. "I truly believe her spirit lives on, even if she is not sitting with us today. Emmie asked me the other day . . ."

"Hi, Dadda," Emmie said sweetly waiving.

Jack waved at his young daughter. "Hi, Baby," he said, and tears flooded his eyes. He suppressed a sob. "Where was I? Oh yes, Emmie asked me the other day if her mommy was an angel, now. Yes, sweet girl. Your mommy is an angel. Even in her death, Claire was able to give life to others." Jack looked down at his paper and paused. "You see, Claire's organs were donated to individuals in need all across the country. Claire's heart saved a young woman in

St. Louis who has been on the transplant list for two years. Claire's lungs went to a teenage boy in California who was not expected to live but three more months. And her beautiful, beautiful eyes were given to a mother in Florida, who can now see because of Claire's gift. But most of all, Claire would be over the moon with joy to know that her kidneys saved a woman she considered a friend." Jack looked at Reese and smiled.

The crowd turned toward the back of the church. Reese waved gently as tears streamed down her face.

"So, today, as we bury the love of my life and the mother to my child, never forget that she *is* an angel and that she lives on through those she saved."

EPILOGUE

SHE SLOWLY WALKED UP THE COBBLESTONE driveway, inhaling and exhaling deeply. She froze when she heard laughter coming from behind the home. Fear crept up her spine, and panic filled her throat. She leaned forward and held her knees. "I can't do this," she said aloud. As she whipped around and dashed toward her car, she ran into the most handsome man she had ever seen. His phone made a cracking noise as it hit the sidewalk.

"Crap,' he said as he bent down. "The screen cracked."

"I'm so sorry," Reese replied embarrassed. Then she burst into tears.

"Hey. Hey, it's okay. It was an accident. Don't cry. It's no big deal. I wasn't watching where I was going."

"No. It's not that, well not only that," she wailed between sobs. "I just can't do this. They all sound so happy, and I can't just walk in there and remind them of . . . She's dead, and I'm alive . . . and, oh God."

He studied her face with curiosity. "Oh, you must've been a friend of Claire's," he said, patting her shoulder. "I know it's sad that she's gone, but this is a celebration of life ceremony. We're all here to remember the good times with her." He paused. "It's okay to cry, but if you were Claire's friend, then she wouldn't want you to be sad. She's in a good place. And she would want you here, with her family."

Reese raised her head to meet his eyes, "I know. You're right. It's just . . ."

"Besides, I'd like to keep talking to you," he said with a wink.

A small laugh escaped her, and she rolled her eyes. *Is he seriously hitting on me, now?*

"So, are you coming or leaving?" he asked with a mischievous smile.

"I'm . . ." She took a step to the side to move around him.

"Reese, you came. I'm so glad you're here," Jack said as he walked toward them.

"Reese?" the handsome guy asked. "As in the Reese that has Claire's kidney?"

"One in the same," Reese said, wiping away her remaining tears. "Hi Jack," Reese called.

"You met my brother?" he asked.

"Your brother?" she said, confused.

Jack gently punched Nolan in the shoulder, and they embraced in a hug. Reese couldn't believe she didn't see the resemblance before. They both had wavy brown hair and green eyes. The only differences were that Nolan stood a foot shorter and was more muscular than Jack.

"Man, it's good to see you again bro. How are ya doing?" Nolan asked.

"Doing fairly good. Every day seems to be a little easier. It's still hard without Claire. I miss her every day."

Jack turned his attention to Reese. "I'm so glad you could make it, Reese." He held his hand out.

Reese accepted his hand, and they shook. "Thank you for the invite, Jack. That was sweet of you to remember me for this special moment."

Nolan raised one eyebrow. "Why don't you tell my darling little brother here that you were just leaving?"

Jack looked confused. "Leaving?"

Reese shot Nolan a dirty look. "I . . . I'm sorry Jack." Tears flooded her eyes again.

"Why? Reese, Claire would want you here. We *all* want you here," Jack said.

"Jack, I'm just a reminder that she's gone. I wouldn't be alive if she weren't dead. It's just . . . I don't know. It's not fair." Sobs escaped her lips again. "It's not fair that she's gone, and I'm still here. Her family doesn't want to be reminded of that."

Jack wrapped his arms around her in a hug. "Reese, you *are* our family now, and you're wrong. Everyone wants to see you. You didn't kill Claire. She was already gone, and I know my Claire. She'd be happy that she was able to help you."

She looked up at Jack and saw his love for Claire shining from his eyes. *How does he do that? How does he look at me and not feel resentment?* "If you're sure, it'll be okay . . ." she said hesitantly.

"Sure, I'm sure," he said with a smile and a pat. "Now wipe those tears and follow me to the backyard. I hope you're hungry. We're grilling a ton of food."

"And for the record, I definitely want you to stay," Nolan said.

Reese looked at him critically. She almost forgot he was standing there.

"Easy there, Tiger," Jack said with a smile. "Today's all about celebrating Claire—it's not a chance for you to go on the prowl." He turned to Reese and gave her a crooked smile. "You have to watch out for this one. He's trouble."

"Trouble! Me?" Nolan winked at Reese again.

Reese inhaled a deep breath and wiped her hands on her pants. *He's definitely trouble*, she thought as she followed Jack.

THE CIRCLE CONTINUES . . .

Look for *Family Circle: Reese Sanders* in 2022!

For Reese Sanders, life has never been idealistic. She was adopted as a baby, and although she had loving parents, she still felt a void that she hoped to fill in finding her birth mother, but then, Reese's life takes an unexpected turn when she needs a kidney transplant. God provides for her needs in an unexpected way, as the death of her friend Claire supplies the life-saving kidney she needs. Dealing with survivors' guilt, Reese struggles to understand her new, spiritual connection to Claire, and just as Reese finally focuses on discovering her birth parents, she endures a physical and emotional assault, from which she isn't sure she'll ever recover. In an onslaught of struggle and strife, can Reese survive the turmoil?

Made in the USA
Coppell, TX
16 January 2022

71704929R00125